TRIBAL LAW

LORI BEASLEY BRADLEY

S hannon Duncan got out of her new Jeep Cherokee and smiled sadly at the tract of cedar-strewn land around her.

She took a deep breath of the warm morning air as she unlocked the sturdy padlock and unwrapped the chain to release the twelve-foot metal farm gate, securing her property from local trespassers. A strong breeze blowing down from the White Mountains ruffled her sandy-blonde hair and carried the sharp, green scent of the cedars into her nose. Somewhere above her head, a lonely bird of prey called, like the obligatory bird in every old western movie she'd ever seen.

She took a deep breath and closed her eyes as she saw herself again as a western pioneer fresh off a wagon train from the east. Shannon had grown up watching westerns on television like Gunsmoke and The Big Valley. She'd grown up on a farm in the Midwest and had always dreamed about having her own cabin in the mountains where she could imagine herself in those olden days.

She'd moved to Arizona in her late teens when her parents relocated due to her father's work and met her husband Ken while taking classes at Arizona State to become a teacher. Ken had received his degree, but Shannon had put her education on hold while she took a retail job to support them. She'd taken classes off and on over the years but never finished more than her Associates in general studies.

After fifteen years at Wal-Mart, she finally wrote the book she'd always promised herself she'd write and self-published. In the high desert, this property was going to be her writing retreat someday where she'd write the great American novel that would make her famous. She smiled to herself. Yeah, right as if that was ever going to happen.

This piece of property had been her dream for years. Shannon thought it had been her husband Ken's dream too, but she found out the hard way it hadn't been. In reality, she supposed Ken hadn't wanted the Arizona high-desert property at all, and he hadn't wanted Shannon either.

Shannon closed her eyes and tried to shut out the horrible memory of the night a week before when she'd been preparing a celebratory meal of T-bones, salad, and baked potatoes to share with her husband, Ken.

It should have been the beginning of the life they'd planned for. Maybe it was really just the one she'd planned for. Perhaps he'd never wanted a secluded cabin in the mountains at all, and she'd pushed him into the dream she'd had for herself.

The rapid knocking of a woodpecker on a tree trunk somewhere reminded Shannon of the knocking on her door that night, and she jerked her head up to stare around at the breeze blowing the cedars. It had been Ken's friend Dale Eubanks knocking at the door. Dale had become Ken's close companion over the past year, but Shannon hadn't suspected how close until that horrible night.

"Hi, Dale," she said in confusion when she opened the door of the three-bedroom ranch house she and Ken had shared in Buckeye, Arizona, since they'd happened upon it ten years earlier while out on a drive and fallen in love with it. "Ken's not home from work yet."

"I know," he said uneasily as he walked in through the door Shannon held open. "I came to talk to you, actually."

"Me? What could you possibly have to talk to me about?" Shannon asked in confusion as she thought. "Is it about his birthday? Do you want to plan something special with me for him? We usually spend his birthday weekend up on the property."

Shannon watched the small-framed man stare around her living room where a forty-eight-inch television stood on a console table beside the gas fireplace with the latest episode of The First Forty-eight in full color on the wide, high definition screen. The room smelled of the charred meat and fresh bread of the meal she'd been preparing, and Dale's intrusion irritated Shannon. This was her big surprise for Ken, and Dale Eubanks had no part in it.

"Smells good in here," he said as he turned back to Shannon. "Must be something special if you're broiling steaks in the middle of the week."

"It is," Shannon said with irritation, and she didn't intend to elaborate. Dale Eubanks didn't have any right to know their personal business. "What did you want to talk to me about, Dale?" If she could get him to spit it out, maybe she could get him out of the house before Ken got home from the school, where he taught math and science.

Dale's eyes bored into Shannon, and she became uncomfortable. "You know Ken and I have grown close over the past several months, don't you, Shannon?" He dropped down into an overstuffed chair. "Do you have any idea how close?"

The color drained from Shannon's face with Dale's tone and the insidious grin on his weasel-like face. "What are you talking about?"

"You can't possibly think we've really been playing poker all those nights," he said, and the smile spread. "Though I suppose you could say we were poking ... one another."

Oh, my lord. What's he trying to say? Shannon felt her

cheeks begin to burn. She'd wondered if Ken was having an affair, but she'd never imagined it would be with Dale--a man. What kind of failure as a wife was she to lose her husband to another man?

Tears of rage and humiliation stung Shannon's eyes as she stumbled to the brown, velour couch. "You're lying," she mumbled. "Is this some sort of sick joke you two have cooked up? If it is, I don't find it funny."

"It's no joke, honey," Dale sneered. "Ken is mine now, and I think you should be moving along."

"Moving along?" Shannon gasped as she stared at the man sitting in her living room with a triumphant smile on his face. "What the hell are you talking about?"

"Ken and I have plans, Shannon," he said, "and you're not part of them. I came over today to tell you because Ken is a sweetheart and didn't want to hurt you with the truth about us." He shrugged his narrow shoulders and stared at her with his beady dark eyes. "I tried to tell him it would be best just to tell you in one quick cut. It would be better for both of you, but you know how he is. He doesn't even like to take the hook out of the fish's mouth because he doesn't want to cause it pain."

They both stared toward the fireplace and went quiet when they heard the garage door opening. A car pulled in, parked, and the garage door rolled back down. A car door opened and closed, and then Ken opened the door and walked into the compact, galley kitchen.

"Something smells good," her husband said in a cheerful tone as he stepped into the living room after dropping his lunchbox onto the counter. "What are you doing here, buddy?" he said to Dale but settled into an uneasy silence when he saw the dazed look on Shannon's face.

Dale stood and turned to face Ken. "It was time to tell her and get this all into the open, Kenny."

Shannon's mouth fell open, and her eyes went wide. He

hates being called Kenny. Does he really let the little twerp call him that when he'd never let me? He told me never to call him Kenny because that's what the bullies at school called him when he was a kid, and he hated it.

Ken glanced at Shannon for only a moment before turning to Dale. "I told you it wasn't the time for that," he snapped at Dale, "and that I'd handle it when it was."

Shannon recognized that tone and wanted to smile at Dale, but she couldn't. She stood and walked to her gaping husband. "Dale here has been telling me that the two of you have plans." She swung her hand and landed a stinging slap on Ken's cheek. "I hope the two of you will be very happy together." Shannon bent and picked up the plastic tackle box she'd prepared earlier that afternoon and dropped it onto the dining room table before storming to their bedroom. "This was supposed to be a surprise," she said, and her eyes flashed to Dale. "but I think Dale here has certainly one-upped me in that department."

As she stuffed clothes into a suitcase, Shannon could hear the men arguing in the living room.

"But she's not much of a wife to you anymore, Kenny," Dale whined. "You said she seldom cooks a meal for you anymore and hasn't pleased you in bed for a long time."

Shannon swiped tears from her face as the aromas of her special dinner filled the room. *Well, I guess you can do the cooking for him now, Dale, and it sounds like you've been taking care of the other department for a while now,* so go ahead and have at it. I'm out of here.

Shannon marched through the living room and into the warm kitchen with her suitcase clutched in her trembling hand. She turned off the oven and took the tray with two large Idaho potatoes out, and set it beside the plate of fresh yeasty rolls.

"Steaks are in the warming oven," Shannon snapped as she went to the bookcase where they kept the fireproof box with their personal papers, "and there are salads in the fridge." She rummaged through a box and took out the deed to the retirement property they'd bought in the foothills of the White Mountains a few years ago and the title to her old Tahoe. She shook the papers at Ken. "I'm taking these." She nodded toward the tackle box open on the table. "What's in there more than covers them."

Ken opened the tackle box and picked up one of the ten neatly wrapped stacks of hundred-dollar bills from the plastic box, staring at Shannon in confusion. "Where did this come from?"

"That was my big surprise, Kenny," Shannon said as she watched her husband's face pale at the use of the name, and she stuffed the papers into her purse as she fished for her keys. "I took my lottery ticket in today, and I hit big for a change if you can believe that."

They'd been buying lottery tickets for years and had savings accounts in separate banks. He would put his winnings into his account, and she did the same. It had been a fun game, and they'd used their meager winnings to make improvements on their retirement property every year. They had always joked about hitting a big one and being able to retire early but never expected it to happen.

Shannon had been so excited when the ticket had hit that morning. It hadn't been the mega prize of hundreds of millions, but it wasn't her usual ten or twenty dollars either. She was a bona fide millionaire even after they'd taken the taxes out and reduced the amount because she wanted her winnings in a lump sum and not dribbled out over twenty-five years. She'd taken the check to the bank from the state lottery office, deposited it, and taken out a hundred thousand dollars in cash to present to Ken along with their special dinner.

"It wasn't the big one," she admitted as she watched Dale finger the bundles of cash, "but I got most of the numbers and the bonus, so we--I," she corrected with a glare at Dale, "can retire and build my cabin in the mountains. Dale thinks you want him to move in here with you," Shannon spat, "so have at it. I'm out of here." Shannon moved toward the door, towing her suitcase

"Are you gonna let her just walk out of here with your money, Kenny?" Dale gasped. "Half of that lottery money is ours--yours. You can't just let her walk away with it. Money like that would pay for our beach house in Mexico and set us up for the rest of our lives down there just the way we always talked about." He stared at Ken, and when hee husband refused to move, he charged at Shannon and grabbed her around the neck in a chokehold. It surprised Shannon that the wiry little man possessed such strength.

Dale tightened his hold, and the light began to blur as Dale's strong fingers cut off the blood flow to her brain, and Shannon slumped toward the floor.

"Let her go, Dale," Ken yelled as he rushed to pull his lover off his wife. "It was her ticket. I still have mine here in my wallet."

"But she's your wife," Dale gasped as he let go of Shannon, and she stumbled away, gasping and coughing. "What's hers is yours--at least half of it anyway, and you should get it before she gets away and hides it somewhere."

Ken snorted. "This isn't the nineteenth century, Dale. A woman can have her own money without her husband's permission."

"But Arizona is a community property state, Ken," Dale continued, "and half of anything she has belongs to you too."

Shannon straightened up and glared at Dale. "You can have that half of my marriage," she said and nodded toward Ken, who stood with the tackle box of cash in his hands, "and my half of this damned house, but that's all you're ever gonna get of mine, asshole." Shannon picked up her suitcase with tears streaming down her red face, stormed out the door, and slammed it behind her.

The next week blurred in Shannon's mind. She remembered driving into Phoenix from Buckeye, checking into a hotel along the I-17, and crying herself to sleep. She woke the next morning to her cell phone ringing but didn't answer it when she saw Ken's name on the caller ID. She showered, dressed, had breakfast in the lobby, and drove her Tahoe to the first car dealership she came to, where she traded it in for the newest four-wheel drive vehicle on the lot. She liked the new Jeep Cherokee and thought it would be a good vehicle for the mountains and rugged unpaved roads bordering her property.

After going through her hastily stuffed suitcase, Shannon treated herself to a shopping spree and bought new jeans, sweaters, socks, and boots for the season coming up. It was late summer in the valley and still hot, but the land in the mountains sat at about six thousand feet in elevation and would be much cooler. The fall would be upon her in no time, and it wasn't unusual to see snow at that elevation in mid to late September. Shannon thought she should be prepared.

Her trip up the mountain had been bittersweet. She'd lunched at a cafe she and Ken had frequented over the years and checked into a favorite hotel. Shannon loved the green in the White Mountains and had looked forward to their trips to visit their property. They'd fenced five acres of the place a year after purchasing it and kept a travel trailer there after they'd installed a septic system and water tank. They'd made plans to build a cabin and live off-grid after their retirement in two years. Their big purchase this year was going to be an array of solar panels. They already had three on top of the travel trailer to power it and the water tank's pump.

She was here now, but she was alone. Could she really do this all by herself? Ken and she were supposed to be doing this together. She thought it had been their dream. How could she have been so wrong?

2

Sam Sweetwater parked his work truck behind the shiny, new Jeep and got out. The woman at the gate didn't turn, and it surprised him to find her alone. Sam had met with Ken Duncan and his wife several times over the years since they'd purchased the remote property in the foothills of the White Mountains, but this was the first time Shannon had come up from the valley without her husband.

"Hey, Mrs. Duncan," he called to get her attention, "you gonna drive on in, or do you want to talk out here?"

She turned, and Sam thought he saw a sadness in her usually bright, blue eyes. "Hi, Mr. Sweetwater," she answered with a forced smile on her pretty, pale face as the breeze blew her dark blonde hair. "Thanks for coming out on such short notice. I just got here too." She pushed open the gate and returned to her vehicle. "I'll pull in, and we can talk at the camper." Before she got in the Jeep, she added, "You can just call me Shannon. The Mrs. Duncan part doesn't really apply anymore."

Her fancy new Jeep started and rolled through the open gate toward the travel trailer parked in a stand of cedars. Sam climbed into his big Ford and followed.

I wonder what happened with those two? Their relationship had always seemed so solid, but who can tell with whites. It was probably a money thing. It usually was. White or red, it made no difference. Money problems ruined relationships.

Sam's marriage to Freda White Owl had ended after only five years, and it was because Freda said Sam didn't make enough money digging holes in the ground for people. In the fifteen years since their divorce, Sam's business, Sweetwater Excavation, had grown, and he was one of the most prosperous businessmen on or off the Zuni reservation. His second wife, Karla, a teacher at the reservation school, had been killed in an automobile accident with a drunk driver, and Sam missed her terribly.

Sam was Zuni, an ancient tribe that traced its roots back thousands of years to the mysterious Anasazi. He'd been born on the Zuni reservation in Apache County. Still, after Karla's death without any children, he'd purchased some property off the reservation and moved with his mother, Sylvia, into a new doublewide mobile home. Sylvia had chafed at moving away from her friends on the reservation, but the brand-new house with its clean, modern appliances in the spacious kitchen, new carpet, and a private bathroom off her bedroom had changed her mind.

Sylvia took care of the house, though she nagged Sam to find a new wife to take care of the house and his needs as a man. She acted as his secretary and kept the books for Sweetwater Excavations. He wished she didn't try to run his life as well, but he couldn't do much about that. He was pushing sixty. Sylvia treated him like he was still a teenager with a curfew and continually pushed him into the company of single Native women she thought suitable for the businessman he'd become and the wife of the Tribal Governor she wanted him to be. She told Sam he had a responsibility to set a good example to the younger men of the Tribe, and having a good Native woman at his side was a part of that responsibility.

Proper Zuni men married women from within their tribe—not white bitches who were only after a share of the monthly casino revenues.

"You'd probably call down my ancestors to come and take my scalp if I started going around with the pretty white woman getting out of that Jeep. Wouldn't you, Sylvia?" Sam mumbled to himself with a smile as he parked his truck and got out.

Shannon unlocked the travel trailer and began carrying plastic bags filled with things she'd picked up from Walmart out of her Jeep. "Looks like I'm gonna be stuck in this horrible thing for a while," she said with a smile and a shrug of her bare, freckled shoulders. It was warm, and she wore a tank top over her full breasts, jeans over her shapely ass, ankle boots on her feet, and a cowboy hat to shade her face.

To Sam, she looked like one of the hundreds of white, cowboy-wannabe tourists who swarmed to the cooler White Mountains in the Summer months to escape the triple-digit heat of the valley below. They also spent their money in the Native-owned tourist shops and businesses like his, so Sam couldn't complain. Very little was crafted by Native artisans these days. It was all cheap reproductions imported from China, and Sam hated seeing it being touted as Native made. It made him feel cheap and dishonest, though he had nothing to do with the tourist traps selling the junk.

"Let me help you with that," Sam said as he took a case of bottled fruit juice and carried it into the travel trailer.

"Would you like some?" she asked, nodding to the case of juice. "I have ice made in the freezer."

"Sure, or just water if you have it. I try to avoid the sweet stuff as much as I can, " he said, patting his belly as he grinned. Sam glanced around the trailer and noticed her suitcase by the unmade bed and new clothes with the tags still on them, poking from the narrow closet door. He also saw the deed to the property spread out on the table in the kitchen.

The place smelled musty and dusty though the windows were open, and Sam thought she'd only opened it for the first time last night, after months of sitting empty. He couldn't remember the last time they'd been up here together, causing him to wonder again what had happened between the two of them.

"If you open the lawn chairs, I'll bring it out," she said with a smile on her pretty face. "The shaded outside is cooler than in this stuffy tin box."

He had to agree and stepped back outside, taking a deep breath of the cooler air. "Will Mr. Duncan be joining us?" Sam asked hesitantly.

"No," Shannon replied in a soft voice, and Sam saw her hands tremble from where he stood in the shade of the swaying cedars as she took tall, plastic tumblers from the cabinet above the sink, "Ken won't be coming here anymore."

"I'm sorry to hear that, ma'am."

"Thanks," she said uneasily before continuing. "I saw Mr. Miller in town yesterday, and he's going to be setting up the cabin shell for me the week after next if you can get the ground all set and the blocks delivered." She twisted a plastic ice cube tray and transferred the cubes into the tumblers before refilling them with water from a bottle and returning them to the small freezer compartment in the trailer's refrigerator.

Sam opened two chairs he found propped next to the trailer and dusted them off. He set up a small table between them. "So, Fred's selling you one of those modular things of his?"

"Yeah," she said as she handed Sam a tumbler filled with ice and water. "One of the ones with the siding that looks like redwood logs and is in an L-shape with a bedroom section added to the front. Ken and I had been looking at them for several years but went back and forth between one of those and just building a custom cabin," she hesitated as she sat and took a sip of juice from her glass, "but now it's a matter of practicality. The shell will be faster to set up than finding a contractor and building from scratch." She rolled her eyes and grinned as she nodded toward the travel trailer. "I don't think I could stand that tin can for the time it would take to build either. I'll just have to find someone to finish the inside of Fred's shell the way I want it."

Sam smiled. "That's easy enough. If you've got the money, my crew and I can do almost anything you might need inside, from paint to tile and custom cabinetry."

"Money won't be a problem," Shannon sighed. "I guess I need some excavation work done before they can set the thing up. Have you worked with Mr. Miller and his buildings before?"

"I have," he said and stood. "Why don't you show me where you want it and tell me what you have in mind. Ken and I talked about it before, so I already have a general idea about where he wanted the cabin."

Shannon's face fell when Sam mentioned her husband's name, and he made a mental note to avoid doing that again. Along with his excavating, Sam was a decent carpenter, and if he could get her business to do all the finish work needed on this cabin project, it could see him and his crew through the slower winter months approaching.

Sam walked with Shannon around the property, and she showed him where she thought the house should go in relation to the septic and water tanks, where she wanted to install her solar panels, her garden, her chicken coop, and possibly even a greenhouse. All of that would certainly see him and his crew through the winter months, and Sam pounced on it before she could find someone else in the area to do the work.

"You're planning to be totally self-sufficient out here, then?" he asked with a broad smile. "That's a lot of work for a woman on her own, Mrs. Duncan.'

Shannon grinned. "As much as I can be, but I draw the

line at cows and goats. My milk and cheese will have to come from the grocery store in town."

Sam shook his head. "Sounds like a lot of work to me even without the milking."

"Women on the reservation have been doing it forever, haven't they?" she asked in a serious tone. "Just because I'm white doesn't mean I can't do hard work if I need to."

"I didn't mean it like that," he said apologetically.

Shannon gave him a warm smile and shrugged. "Gonna have to fill my days with something. I like gardening and preserving the produce. I grew up on a farm in the Midwest, so I've done it all before."

"It's gonna be lonely out here all by yourself."

"I'll have my chickens to keep me company, and I'll probably go to the county animal shelter and get a dog and a cat." She grinned. "They can help me with my writing, as well."

Sam raised an eyebrow. "A dog and a cat?"

"A cat to keep down the mice and a dog to warn me about rats and snakes," Shannon said with a grin and added, "the two-legged kind especially."

"Oh," he said and returned her grin. He liked her grin. Shannon might be a few years older than him, but her child-like grin went to her eyes and made them sparkle. "You're a pretty woman, so I suppose that could become an issue if people know you're staying out here alone."

Shannon rolled her eyes. "Thanks, you're not bad looking yourself, Mr. Sweetwater. I bet you have women all over the county calling you to help them with their—eh--plumbing problems."

It was Sam's turn to roll his eyes, and he chuckled. He'd forgotten about her wicked sense of humor.

"Unfortunately, everyone knows my mother screens my calls at the office." He took a pen from the front pocket of his T-shirt and a business card from his wallet. He scribbled something on the back before handing Shannon the card. "I put my personal cell number on the back so you can contact me directly if you need anything."

"Thanks," she said and slipped the card into the back pocket of her jeans. "I'll put it in my phone. When do you think you can get started, and what do you estimate it's going to cost?"

He needed to be careful here. This was a smart woman. He remembered her keeping close tabs on the money she and her husband spent on the place. "It depends on how much you want me and my guys to do," he said. "I can do the excavation and the concrete work for the cabin, and we can do the finish work too, electrical, plumbing, drywall, and painting. Like I said before—pretty much everything you'll need to get the cabin livable."

"That would be awesome," she sighed. "I love one-stop shopping. Can I give you a check for ten thousand to get things started?" she added when Sam didn't reply right away, "Like a retainer to work from, and I'll give you more as the work progresses and you need more."

She'd said the money wouldn't be a problem, but he hadn't thought it would be this easy.

"Yeah, that would be great," he said, trying to keep the excitement from his voice, "and I'll write you up a detailed estimate of everything we've discussed tonight and bring it by in the morning along with my crew and equipment to get this job rolling. Do you have the spec sheet or blueprints for the cabin shell you're getting, or do I need to pick them up from Fred?"

"I have them in the Jeep. You have no idea what a load that takes off me," Shannon said as they walked back to the shade of the cedars. "I know you do good work, Mr. Sweetwater, and I trust you'll do what you say you will." She went into the trailer and returned with her checkbook. "I wouldn't hand over this kind of money to just anybody, you know."

"Call me, Sam, please. Mr. Sweetwater was my grandfather, and he hasn't been a part of my life for a very long time."

"All right, Sam," she said uneasily as she tore the check from the checkbook and handed it to him. "Here you go. I look forward to working with you."

Sam took the check and studied it. Only her name appeared on it, and Sam wondered again about what had happened to their marriage. The number on the check was over nine hundred. Maybe she was like his mother and had always handled the money in the marriage. Or had she opened a new account and had the checks printed with a high number to give the impression of a long-time account.

He sure hoped this check was good, but it wouldn't be a problem to check. There was a branch in town, and he had an account there. One of the girls would check it out for him to make certain it was good before he deposited it. He could probably even get her to tell me about how much she had to work with, so he didn't get in over his head with this project.

For the first time, he noticed that Shannon stood with her hand out, expecting to shake his and make their business arrangement official. Embarrassed, he took her hand and shook it. "I look forward to working with you as well, Shannon. I'll be back in the morning with my crew to get started on the dirt work."

Now he was embarrassed that he'd been holding her hand too long and released it. She gave him a warm smile, and a thought struck him. "Did you and—eh--your husband ever have any problems about buying this land?" He glanced off across the swaying meadow grass and breathed in the rich aroma of the cedars. "This is considered sacred land to some of my people on the reservation. They used to dance here for religious observances, and I know there were some very upset people when they came here and had to drive around the fence to get to the dance site."

Shannon's mouth fell open, and her eyes went wide. "I

don't think anyone ever mentioned anything. I'm sure the title company would have said something if there had been an issue like that." He watched her eyes go to the sturdy farm gate. "People have been coming on my property to dance?"

"To celebrate certain cycles of the moon," Sam admitted nervously. "The dance site is at the back end of this property, and I don't think they've ever bothered your trailer or anything."

Shannon shrugged and smiled. "It's a big piece of property," she said. "If they want to come here and dance for religious ceremonies, I guess it's all right."

"I'll let the Tribal Council know," Sam said before turning toward his truck. "I'm sure they'll be glad to hear it."

※ 3 *※*

Shannon watched the man walk away and wondered why she'd never noticed how handsome he was before. Sam Sweetwater had done work for them several times over the years, but she'd never really paid much attention to his looks. Was it because he was Native, and she'd never given much thought to Native men?

No, it was because she thought she'd had a happy marriage and didn't need to look elsewhere. Boy, had she been wrong.

Shannon watched Sam's truck cause fine dust to billow into the clear air as he drove away and then returned to the camper to put away the rest of her groceries. After spending two nights in the hotel, meeting with Fred Miller in town, and purchasing the cabin shell, Shannon had driven to the property and opened up the camper to air out. She and Ken hadn't been up in over six months.

That in itself should have been a clue to Shannon that something was amiss in her marriage. Ken had wanted to come up the mountain at every opportunity, but those opportunities had become fewer and fewer over the past year as his fishing and hunting trips with Dale had increased. She should have seen what was going on. Poker games, indeed, and fishing trips without any fish. She was such a fool. What kind of wife had she been not to have made the connection?

Shannon took a deep breath and dashed tears from her face as she stacked canned goods on shelves and found room in the cramped cabinets for boxes of cereal and Bisquik. She carried an armload of bathroom supplies into the tiny alcove and found room for them beneath the sink. Shannon hung the new towels on the rod over the toilet and stuffed new washcloths into a drawer. Shannon picked up the old rug in front of the shower unit and carried it to the door, where she tossed it outside along with the mud-stained one from the kitchen and all of Ken's things she'd found during her rummaging.

It's time to start fresh, and this old camper is as good a place as any to begin.

The poor cell reception in the area had put an end to Ken's calls and texts, at least. While in her hotel room in town, she'd listened to his messages and read the texts, pleading with her to understand and begging her forgiveness for Dale's poor behavior before she left the house.

She'd deleted them all and hadn't replied. Had Ken expected her to respond or to forgive him for that humiliation? What he'd done wasn't understandable and certainly not something she was ready to forgive. Would Ken have expected her to forgive him if he'd been stepping out on her with another woman? Would he have been willing to forgive her had she been stepping out on him?

Shannon fixed herself a bowl of oatmeal and sat down at the table with a pad of grid paper and a ruler to sketch in her ideas for the finished cabin. As she worked, Shannon's mind went back to the muscular tawny-skinned shoulders beneath the tight white T-shirt, the long black hair that shone with blue highlights in the sun, and the shapely behind of Sam Sweetwater as he walked away. She felt her cheeks flush as she wondered what his full, dark lips would taste like, and she smiled. It was her first real smile in days, and it hurt her face. Tears blurred her vision of the paper, and Shannon dropped her pencil.

She had to get hold of herself. Her marriage was over, but she had a new life here to look forward to. Sam's face came into her head, and she smiled, remembering the dimples in his burnished cheeks when he smiled at her.

He has a great smile. She should sketch it.

She picked up the pencil and continued to draw. She penciled in the bathroom fixtures and the kitchen cabinets and appliances. On another sheet of paper, Shannon sketched a wall with a large fireplace with a heavy wood mantle and bookcases on either side. This was her chance to fulfill her dream of what she wanted the cabin to be, and she used her long-suppressed artistic abilities to put those dreams on paper. Shannon could picture a large painting of the mountains mounted above the mantle. Maybe she'd paint one.

Shannon had loved art as a child, and instructors told her she had a good eye for detail. She'd minored in drawing and painting in college, but her first boyfriend there hadn't been supportive and teased her about her 'little pictures.' When she entered her work in some college competitions and failed to place, Peter had laughed and told her she was destined to be a true starving artist if she pursued painting, so she'd put her paints and easel away. She still had a good eye, and people had always raved about her home decorating abilities.

She'd sketched a little for Ken, but their tastes were different, and Shannon had limited her artistic pursuits to painting walls and hanging pieces she collected at craft sales. She was adamant about purchasing only original art for her homes but spent only what she could afford at the time.

She supposed she could afford more now and grinned to herself. She winced, thinking about the picture on velvet of dogs in cowboy hats seated around a poker table Ken had insisted on buying at a yard sale. That would probably have been his choice to go above the mantle.

Not in my dream house, buddy, Shannon thought with a grin.

❦

Sam walked in the house to the aroma of peppers and pork simmering in the kitchen. His mother, if nothing else, was an excellent cook.

"How was your day, Sammy?" Sylvia Sweetwater called from the kitchen. "Did you get that job Fred called about?"

Sam walked into the kitchen, where his mother was setting the table. Her silver hair hung in long braids, and she wore a loose T-shirt over a brightly colored three-tiered skirt. Heavy silver and turquoise jewelry adorned her neck, ears, and wrists. A silver concho belt snugged her slender waist, and soft leather boots covered her feet.

In her youth, Sylvia Sweetwater had been beautiful, but age lines now marred her face, and years of cigarette smoking had claimed her teeth a decade ago. She only wore her dentures when she went out in public with her gentleman friend, Nathan, or had visitors.

He handed Sylvia the deposit slip from the bank where he'd verified Shannon's healthy account and kissed her wrinkled cheek. "I got it and then some," he said with a smile. "I think this job might see us through the slow season this winter."

Sylvia handed her son a plate stacked with hot flatbread fresh off the griddle before she looked at the deposit slip. "Ten grand?" she gasped as she studied the white slip of paper. "What do you have to do for this?"

"The dirt work for one of Fred's buildings, a porch and patio on the front, and all the inside finish work to make it livable," Sam said with a smile. "Maybe even more. She's talking about solar panels, a big chicken coop in the back, and maybe a greenhouse too."

"She?" Sylvia said with a raised brow as she set an enameled Paula Deen pot of green chili stew on the table. "What woman around here has that kind of money to throw around?" Sylvia sat and forked a piece of bread from her plate. "A white one, no doubt."

"Mrs. Duncan, the woman who bought the old dance grove on the south edge of the reservation," Sam said nervously as he ladled stew over his bread and waited for the explosion he knew would come from his mother. Sylvia Sweetwater was a racist of the third degree when it came to whites.

Sylvia slapped her fork onto the table. "That's not a job you can take, Samuel," she hissed at her son. "That's sacred Tribal land, and whites have no right to live there." She pushed her chair away from the table, stood, and began to pace around the spacious kitchen. "You can't help some white bitch with money defile our sacred land. I won't allow it."

"Are you going to feed Teddy and Micah's families this winter and cover their rent when I have no work for them?" Sam countered. "This is going to be a big job, Mother, and we need the work."

"Our ancestors are buried on that land, Samuel. You must refuse this job."

"Not on the five acres where the house is going, they're not." He got up and took a beer from the refrigerator. "I've put in a septic tank, a long driveway, and drilled fence post holes without finding remains of any kind. If there are remains on that property, they're somewhere else, not around where she wants to put her cabin."

"What about our sacred seasonal ceremonies, Samuel? They put a gate up to keep us off our sacred land." Sylvia returned to her seat with a can of beer in her hand.

"Mrs. Duncan has no problem with allowing access to the

dance site, Mother. She told me today that it's all right for people to drive back there for the ceremonies."

Sylvia snorted and popped the tab on her can. "How gracious of her," Sylvia sneered. "As if her damned fence ever stopped us."

"Well, there you go," Sam said with a shrug. "There's no reason to cause trouble with Mrs. Duncan, Mother. She can have her cabin, and The Zuni can have their ceremonies."

"There has been a discussion in Council," Sylvia said with a satisfied smile, "about filing a lawsuit to take possession of that land should the whites ever try to move more than that old camper onto it. I think that time has come."

"Mother, you can't be serious. The Duncans bought that land years ago from whites. Why were there never lawsuits filed to claim it by the tribe back then?"

"As if white courts would have paid any heed to a suit by Natives back then," Sylvia hissed at her son. "Anyhow, the man who owned it before these Duncans was married to a Native woman and gave us free access to the land for our ceremonies. He also promised to keep it sacred and never build there. He grazed livestock on it and nothing more," Sylvia said, raising her hands in a dismissive gesture.

"But he sold it to the Duncans and obviously never mentioned any of those stipulations."

Sylvia shook her head as she forked up a bite of stew and bread. "His family sold it after he and his wife died. They never had children, so there was no longer any connection to the tribe."

"Then why didn't the Council file suit then?" Sam asked and emptied his beer.

"We went to the County meeting," Sylvia spat, "but the white bastards told us there was no evidence the land had burials on it and to hold our silly dances on the reservation where we belonged." She took a bite of her food and chewed. "What do you suppose would happen if one of us bought one of their abandoned churches and wanted to build over a forgotten cemetery?" Sylvia swallowed some beer to wash down the spicy pork and peppers. "You'd hear the damned yelling all the way to the state capitol building in Phoenix. That's for certain."

"You're probably right," Sam agreed, "but with no proof of remains on the property, there isn't much ground for a lawsuit."

"You could find proof," Sylvia said hopefully. "You can go off and dig around until you find remains, and then the County and the State will have to award the land to the Tribe like it should have been when they established the damned reservation over a hundred years ago."

"I'll see what I can do, Mother, but I seriously doubt there are burials on that property." Sam scraped a final bite from his plate. "If there were, they would have been found long ago."

Sylvia reached for her son's hand with a smile on her face. "I'm sure you'll do what is right for your tribe, Sammy. You're a good man."

$$4$$

"These are really good," Sam said, studying the sketches he'd picked up from the table in the camper along with the floor plan she'd drawn.

Shannon snatched the sketches from Sam's hand, folded them, and shoved them into the back pocket of her jeans. "Just some doodling I did the other night," she said as she stepped out of the way of Sam's crew members Teddy and Micah, who were unloading cabinets from Home Depot to be installed in the kitchen and bathroom.

Sam stepped around the heavy oak-framed futon Shannon had in the living room area and went to the wall across from it. "We can put an insert in here," he said with a broad smile, "and build that big stone fireplace around it easy enough, and I can build the bookshelves on either side of it just like in your picture." He nodded at the futon. "I can even get golden oak to match your bed there too, but we have to finish the wiring, insulation, and drywall first."

"I really appreciate how hard you guys are working on getting me set up here so quickly. I can't believe it's only been three weeks, and this has been delivered and set up," Shannon said with a giggle. "You have no idea how happy I am to be out of that damned camper."

"I can imagine," Teddy said with a grin on his weathered face. "I'd sleep under the cedars before I'd coop myself up in a tin can like that."

Micah elbowed his older cousin, whose long black hair was pulled back into a ponytail that hung to the middle of his broad shoulders. "Yeah, well, your smell would scare off the coyotes. Miss Shannon doesn't smell as bad as you and wouldn't be safe out here in the open at night."

"I don't know about that," Shannon said with a raised brow, noting her sweaty armpits. The day had turned warm after the early morning frost, and the uninsulated building was warm even with the doors and windows open.

Sam moved Teddy aside. "We'll get the foundation in as soon as we can, so you don't freeze, Shannon, and then we'll get to all this inside work."

"Hey," Teddy said to Sam, "I saw Uncle Nathan and your mom in Home Depot. Did you see them?"

Shannon saw Sam's face darken. "Yeah, we saw 'em," was all he said.

They had been in the bath department giggling together over fixtures when Sylvia and her gentleman friend had walked up behind them.

"So, this is the white interloper on our sacred land?" Sylvia had snapped, ending their pleasant shopping trip.

"Excuse me?" Shannon had said with a shocked expression on her face as she turned to face the older Native couple.

"Mother," Sam had said in a scolding tone. "This is my employer, Shannon Duncan. Shannon, this is my mother Sylvia Sweetwater and her—her gentleman friend--Nathan Tyler."

"Nathan Dog Soldier," the heavy-set man with long, braided gray hair, Native features, and lighter skin said, correcting Sam as he glared at him menacingly. "I'm Nathan Dog Soldier."

Sam rolled his eyes. "Whatever, Nathan," Sam hissed.

Neither offered their hands to Shannon, and she kept hers at her side. "It's nice to meet you."

Sylvia snorted. "It's nice that you're giving my son all that white man's money, but you should leave our land. You have no right there."

"I beg your pardon?" Shannon said uneasily, glancing at Sam. "That land is mine. My former husband and I bought it years ago, and I have a deed registered with the County to prove it."

"White men stole that land from us years ago," Nathan sneered. "It's sacred ceremonial land that belonged to our tribe for eons, and we want it returned to us."

"Nathan," Sam snapped, "you and my mother should go. This is not the place to air your ridiculous political agenda."

Sylvia stepped in front of her son and pointed one of her ringed fingers. "What has this white woman done to turn you against your people, Samuel?" The old Native woman turned to Shannon. "Has she bought you with her white money in her bank or with her white skin and what she has between her legs?"

"Mother, that's enough," Sam hissed as he put his strong hands on his mother's shoulders and turned her around. "Get what you came here for and go home before you cost me my job."

Sylvia grinned at Shannon as she shook Sam's hands off her trembling shoulders. "I've got more than what I came for," she said. "The Council members have made their decision. We are filing suit with the County for the return of our sacred land." She turned back to Sam. "Get what you can from her, son, while you can, because when the Court rules in the Tribe's favor, we'll be taking down the fences she's erected and tearing her garish cabin off our land." The old woman took Nathan's hand and marched away.

"Enjoy your overripe white fruit while you can, Sammy," Nathan said with a giggle over his shoulder.

Shannon had stood in the aisle with her mouth open as the two walked away. "What the hell just happened?" she asked Sam. She gripped the cart filled with plumbing fixtures, drywall screws, and tubs of drywall mud, her legs suddenly feeling like water beneath her.

Sam put a hand on the small of her back. Shannon felt comfort radiating from his touch and leaned into it, perhaps more than she should have. "It's nothing to worry about," he assured her and took his hand away. "It's just my mother and her leaching paramour spouting their racist agenda in public again."

"Can they really take my land?"

"They can try," Sam said, "but there's no proof there were ever any burials on the ground, and in cases like this in the past, there had to be strong archeological proof of remains for the Tribe to regain possession."

They had found Teddy and Micah at the snack bar, eating hotdogs, rolled their carts through checkout, and returned to the cabin to unload. Sam and Shannon hadn't spoken much on the return trip, both deep in thought about the encounter in the store.

Shannon made herself and Sam a sandwich after Teddy and Micah had finished unloading the trucks and left for the day. "Why did I get the impression your mother and Nathan think our relationship is more than strictly professional?" Shannon asked as they walked outside with their food and cans of juice to sit in the shade of the awning Sam and his crew had constructed while the flooring contractor installed vinyl plank tile inside that looked like gray weathered wood planks.

Sam grinned, and his cheeks deepened in color. "I may

have let a few things slip in conversation to give them that impression."

"But we're not ..." Shannon said, wide-eyed.

"I know," Sam said, raising his hand in a defensive posture, "but the two of them are so racist toward whites, I couldn't help myself, and my foolish mother is so set on me running for Tribal Governor. I can't do that if I'm involved with a white woman and the look on her face every time I hinted we were involved sexually was too priceless to resist," Sam said, chuckling deep in his chest.

The dimples in his cheeks when he grinned caused Shannon to smile as well. "Do you think that was a good idea? It's just aggravating an already tense situation if they think I'm living on land they think belongs to your Tribe."

"I know, but I couldn't help myself." His face grew serious again. "Do you find the thought of the two of us as a couple unthinkable?"

"What?" Shannon said, choking on the bite she'd just swallowed.

Was he asking her if she wanted to have more of a relationship? How did she answer that? He had to be playing with her, trying to piss his mother and her boyfriend off at her expense.

"I guess you do," he said with a frown as Shannon coughed. He stuffed the rest of his sandwich in his mouth and chewed. "I meant no offense, Mrs. Duncan." He dropped the empty plate on the chair and marched to his truck.

"Now, what did I do?" Shannon mumbled as she watched Sam's truck throw up dust as he drove away.

༺❀༻

Sam scowled at the road ahead. Did she think she's too good to be with a poor Indian like him? He shook his head. Did just the thought of it make her sick?

Sam pulled his truck into Patsy's, a small bar and burger joint just outside the reservation. Tables outside beneath a sagging lattice awning were full of patrons with baskets of fries and bottles of beer, smoking cigarettes. Arizona law no longer allowed smoking inside buildings outside the reservation, though few at Patsy's recognized the white man's law and lit up inside anyhow.

"Hey, Sam," one of the men called, "you got any work for a strong back like mine and maybe my son's?"

Sam turned to see Paul Crow Feather waiting for a reply. Though most of his earnings ended up here at Patsy's or one of the other bars around the reservation, Paul was a good worker.

"Sure, Paul," Sam said, waving at the man he hired occasionally. "I've got some crates of flagstone being delivered to the job tomorrow. I could use you and your boys to lay a patio for me if you guys have the time."

"At the white bit—eh--lady's cabin on the dance site?" Paul asked uneasily.

Sam lifted his brow. "Is that a problem? If it is, me, Teddy, and Micah can handle it."

"No, man," Paul said, shaking his head, "me and my boys can use some of that cash she's throwing around town like a princess throwing candy in a parade."

Sam saw the dark eyes of the others sitting around the tables staring at him. "You people should all keep in mind that she's throwing all that cash around this community and not somewhere else. She could be buying everything down in the valley at better prices and having it carted up here, but she's not. She's buying everything up here and paying your inflated prices for the goods and services."

"White surtax," a woman laughed, and others joined in.

"Be at my place at seven in the morning with your boys, Paul," Sam said, ignoring the laughter and went inside Patsy's for a beer.

He didn't feel like going home and facing his mother and probably Nathan. Ten years younger than his mother, the man had attached himself to Sylvia and her anti-white causes. He fed her ego with pretty words, and she wined and dined him at the best restaurants in the casinos where he spent her money —the money Sam paid her for doing his bookkeeping and her stipend from the casino as a member of the tribe.

Nathan drove a new Range Rover, and he suspected Sylvia had co-signed for the vehicle. It angered Sam that the man used his mother, but Sylvia was a grown woman and told him more than once to stay out of her affairs. He did, though it didn't stop Sylvia from sticking her nose into his. Her rant in Home Depot wasn't the first time Sylvia had made a public spectacle of herself where Sam and a lady friend were concerned. Now that she'd gotten it into her head that Sam should run for Tribal Governor, he constantly dodged dinners and meetings Sylvia arranged with women she thought would make a good governor's wife.

Why couldn't Sylvia let him live his own life? He knew she was his mother and thought it her duty, but please. He was a grown man and could make his own decisions—especially about the women he dated.

☙❧

Shannon turned off the lights and crawled between the blankets on the futon to get comfortable and watch some television before going to sleep. After Sam's hasty departure, she'd spent the afternoon pushing the cabinets she'd purchased into place in the kitchen area and studied the granite samples the counterman had given her. She'd called him and told him she'd decided on a gray granite with flecks of black and brown in it. She thought the light gray would look good with the white cabinets she'd chosen for the small cabin and the gray tile on the floor. The flecks of brown would highlight the river rock tiles of the fireplace as well, and she might use them on the wall between the counter and the upper cabinets to enhance the rustic appearance of the kitchen. She'd also made room for the appliances scheduled to be delivered the next day.

Sam had agreed with her about using white cabinets in the small space and suggested white or very light pastel colors to paint the drywall they would be installing soon. As much as she loved wood, Shannon didn't want to overpower the small cabin with it. Over the years since purchasing the property, she and Ken had drafted plan after plan for the cabin they wanted for their golden years, tossing out this idea and that one. It saddened Shannon some that she didn't have anyone to share this new adventure with, but she also didn't have to make concessions for anyone either. She could have things exactly how she wanted them without regard to someone else's likes or dislikes.

Shannon was about to turn off the television when a noise in the drive caught her attention. She kicked off the warm blankets, reached for the 357 she kept beneath her pillow and walked barefoot to the door. The headlights of a vehicle blinded her as it pulled up in front of the cabin.

"Who the hell is this?" she mumbled to herself as doors opened, men got out and stepped beneath the newly constructed awning. Shannon cursed herself for not closing and locking the gate after Sam had left the property.

The men walked toward the cabin, and Shannon's hand tightened on the grip of the heavy firearm.

"Good evening, Mrs. Duncan," Nathan Dog Soldier said as he stepped closer to the door. "Aren't you going to be neighborly and invite us in?"

"No, Mr. Tyler," Shannon said, remembering Sam introducing him that way, "I'm not. What do you want?"

"It's Dog Soldier, woman," one of the other Native men snapped in a deep voice. "He's Nathan Dog Soldier, and he's Chief of the Brethren, representing Tribal Law of the Zuni

People of the Reservation. You'll show him the respect he deserves.," the man growled, "or we'll come in and show you what the red men did to mouthy white women back in the day." He grinned and played at shaking his penis at her through his jeans.

Shannon turned the knob on the steel screen door, making certain the deadbolt was engaged. "How nice for you," Shannon said to Nathan. "I was just going to bed, so if you want something, get on with it or come back in the morning."

Nathan jetted forward and grabbed the doorknob. Disappointment etched his features when he found it securely locked. "I'm here representing the Brethren, Mrs. Duncan, the working men of the reservation. We're here to make certain you hire only native men to do work here on the Tribal property from here on out."

"I don't know what you're talking about, Chief," Shannon said with a sneer in her voice. "All my work is being done by Native men—Sam Sweetwater, Teddy, and his cousin Micah White Horse. You know that."

The men behind Nathan chuckled. Sam Sweetwater is a damned Apple," Nathan said with a chuckle, "red on the outside, but white on the inside, and Teddy and Micah are both half-breeds who live off the reservation, married to white women. They've given up their right to be called Native or Brethren, and the Tribe has dropped them from the rolls."

"I'm done with this, Chief. I'm going to bed," Shannon said and pushed the inside door to close.

"Maybe you'd like us to join you," one of the men called.

"We could show you what real native men can do to a white woman in the sack," another added as they all laughed. "I bet I know more tricks than Sam and could make you squeal all night long," one of them called to her.

Shannon raised the pistol for all of them to see. "I suggest you take your band of heathens and get off my property, Chief," Shannon hissed. "Or I'll be forced to deal with the lot of you the way most white women did back in the day and blow your damned heads off."

All the laughing stopped except Nathan's. "You can't shoot us through that metal door, Mrs. Duncan, so you should listen to my terms." Nathan put his arm around the shoulder of one of the men, an intoxicated individual with his long hair in a ponytail. "Paul here and his two sons will be here with Sam tomorrow to lay flagstone for this patio of yours," he said and kicked up some of the fresh sand Sam's men had raked and leveled with his polished boot. "Sam will pay them, but you'll also pay the Brethren through me. You'll be billed twenty-five dollars an hour for each man on the job, and there will always be four Brethren on the job even if there is only one. You will also be billed for ten hours each day even if there is only one hour of work." The men behind Nathan chuckled. "Am I understood, Mrs. Duncan?"

"I don't mind being called a whore," one of the younger men called. "We can start that right now with a little work in your bed."

Shannon had heard enough. She walked to the open window beside the door and raised the pistol to press against the screen. "Get off my property, Mr. Tyler," she said in a calm voice as she aimed over their heads and pulled the trigger.

"Damn, the bitch is shooting at us, Nathan," Paul yelled as he ducked away from Nathan and ran toward the vehicle.

Nathan followed, yelling over his shoulder, "You'll regret this, cunt. You're on Tribal land now and subject to Tribal Law."

"Fuck your Tribal Law and the horse you rode in on," Shannon yelled and pulled the trigger again. " My land is not on your damned Reservation."

She heard glass breaking, and the engine roar to life. The vehicle lurched away from the cabin, and Shannon fired again. More glass shattered as the headlights headed toward the open gate and out onto the road.

Shannon slipped on her dirty sneakers, grabbed a flashlight, and rushed down the drive to close and secure the gate. She didn't want Nathan and his thugs coming back for more fun and games.

S am arrived the next morning to find Shannon's gate closed and locked.

He wondered if she was pissed about the way he'd taken off the day before. He probably shouldn't have done that.

Sam got out of the truck and used the key Ken had given him years ago to unlock the padlock and unchain the gate. He pushed it open, and the two trucks drove up the driveway. Sam smiled when he smelled coffee coming from inside the cabin. His boots crunched on something, and he looked down to see tempered glass scattered on the ground. A chill ran down his spine when he saw the holes in the screen, and he rushed inside where Shannon stood filling mugs from a glass Mr. Coffee pot. She'd obviously made it in the camper and brought it into the cabin for them.

"What the hell happened here?" Sam demanded as he stood at the window, poking his index finger through one of the holes in the screen and sniffing the gunpowder. He turned to Teddy and Micah. "You guys get that glass cleaned up before the truck gets here with the sandstone pallets."

They took the mugs of coffee Shannon offered. "Sure thing, boss," Teddy said and followed his cousin out the door.

Sam grabbed Shannon's wrist. "Tell me what happened."

Shannon swallowed some coffee before answering. "I had a visit from Nathan and some of his Brethren goons last night."

Sam's eyes narrowed, and his brow furrowed at her words. "The Brethren?"

There could be real trouble for her if Nathan brought the damned Brethren into this.

Shannon snorted. "They called him their Chief or some bullshit like that."

Sam rolled his eyes. "Nathan Tyler is a Chief only in his damned dreams." He set the steaming cup in the window and went to Shannon, taking her upper arms in his hands. "Are you all right? Did they hurt you?" he asked in concern.

Shannon leaned into him and rested her sandy blonde head on Sam's shoulder. "I was in the house with the door locked," she said as she slumped into Sam. He could feel her trembling, and he wrapped his arms around her. "He couldn't get in, but he made a lot of demands he thought I'd follow."

Sam pushed her back gently and stared into her blue eyes, brimming with tears. "What kind of demands? I wish you'd called me." He pulled her close again. "I'd have come." Her body felt so good in his arms.

"I know you would have," Shannon said with a sob, and he felt tears wetting his shoulder through his T-shirt.

He was going to kick Nathan's ass for putting her through this. That arrogant prick had gone too far this time, and Sam was going to let him know what he thought about it.

Shannon pulled away and swiped at her eyes. "I was OK," she said and took a long swallow from her mug. "I had my gun and sent him and his pack of hounds running." She nodded at the holes in the screen and grinned. "I guess you're going to have to add a new screen to your to-do list.

They heard the engine of a large truck. "It sounds like the

flagstones are here," Sam sighed, "but the guys I hired yesterday to lay them didn't show this morning."

Shannon emptied her mug and ran a hand through her hair. "Probably because I shot one of them last night."

Sam's mouth fell open. "What?"

"Nathan said the guys with him were supposed to come to work with you today to lay the patio stones and that I was supposed to start paying him for their labor."

"That son-of-a-bitch," Sam snarled as he picked up his mug from the window. "Who the hell does he think he is?"

"Heap big Chief without some of the windows in his truck," Shannon said with a nervous grin as she used her hand to mimic shooting her pistol out the window.

Sam chuckled. "Windows?"

"I know I took out the windshield while it was still parked," Shannon said as she refilled her mug, "and I heard glass breaking again as he and his crew drove away." She took a deep breath and eased herself into one of the empty lawn chairs. "Once I started shooting, I just kept on until the gun was empty." Shannon put the mug to her lips with trembling hands. "I don't know," she sighed, "but I think I hit it three or four times. I hope I didn't hurt anyone."

"What time did this all go down?" Sam asked as he peeked out the window to watch the pallets of stone being lifted off the truck with a wench. "I really wish you'd called me, Shannon."

"It was about eleven," she said. "I'd just turned off the TV to go to sleep when I heard the truck drive up."

"You probably didn't hit anybody," he assured her. "The reservation police would have been here already if you had."

"Great," she sighed and rested her head on the back of the chair to stare up into the ceiling rafters, "the police. I didn't even think about the police. I probably should have called them last night to report what happened."

"Please promise me you'll call me if Nathan ever comes

back here and causes any problems," Sam said, "and definitely call the County Sheriff's Office. They should be made aware. This property isn't the reservation, so it's in their jurisdiction." His eyes flashed back to the holes in the screen. "Is that gun of yours registered, Annie Oakley?"

Shannon grinned. "Yep, it's all legal."

"Good, then I doubt you'll have any problems with the authorities since you're protecting your property and yourself."

"We're gonna get started on this rock, boss," Teddy called from outside.

"Sure, Ted, go ahead. I'm gonna get things started in here."

They heard the men laughing outside, and the truck roll away. "Nathan and his Brethren don't like you and your crew very much, do they?"

Sam furrowed his brow. "Why? What did they say?"

Shannon sipped her coffee and repeated the uncomfortable conversation between her, Nathan, and the men.

Sam shook his head in disgust. "They had no right talking to you that way, Shannon, and I'm sorry my needling of my mother and Nathan put you in that situation."

"It's not your fault," Shannon insisted. "I think Nathan is a greedy old bastard who's on some kind of power trip with these Brethren of his and thought he could scare me into paying his ridiculous price." Shannon reached out and took Sam's hand. "It wasn't about red and white; it was all about green with him, and he thought I'd be an easy mark as a woman out here alone."

Sam smiled and put his other hand over hers. "You set him straight on that account. I don't think he'll be messing with the lady gunslinger again anytime soon."

Sam decided to take a chance, bent close, and kissed Shannon on the lips. She surprised him when she opened her mouth and invited his tongue inside, returning his kiss with enthusiasm. She tasted like coffee, and her body felt great, so close to his. Sam wrapped his arms around her and pulled her close as the kiss deepened.

"Just what exactly are you getting started on in here, boss," Micah said with a giggle as he pressed his face into the metal screen of the door.

Sam looked up to see both men standing at the screen door with big grins on their faces.

"I guess it's time for me to get to work," Sam said to Shannon with an embarrassed grin. He turned to the door where Teddy and Micah stood red-faced and grinning. "Shannon and I are going to install these cabinets," he said. "Why aren't you knuckleheads planting stone?"

By the time the sun had begun to set, and they needed to turn on lights, Shannon had upper and lower cabinets in her kitchen, the vanity installed in the bathroom, and the countertop man had come to measure for the granite. Sam had also installed the toilet, and the appliance store had delivered her stainless steel side-by-side refrigerator, a small, low voltage microwave, and a stacked washer/dryer unit. The reproduction antique cookstove wouldn't arrive for a few more days, but at least Shannon had a place for her food and didn't have to run back and forth between the cabin and the camper every time she wanted a sandwich or use the bathroom.

"This is going to look real nice when Iron Eagle gets that granite installed," Micah said, fingering the samples, "but I'd have probably gone with the black granite instead of the gray."

"Too dark for this little room," Teddy said. "She was right to pick the gray." He winked at Shannon before elbowing his cousin in the ribs. "And it goes with the floor she picked, stupid."

"Yeah," Micah countered, "but I'd have picked darker wood for that too, and then it would have matched the black granite for the counter."

Teddy rolled his tired brown eyes and slapped his cousin on the shoulder. "Good grief, I give up with you, Cuz. Let's get home before our suppers get cold."

Two of the pallets of sandstone had been set, and Shannon had a patio beneath her awning. "You guys did a great job today," Shannon said as she stepped out onto the perfectly even stones, solidly packed together with sandy grout. "This is just as beautiful as I'd imagined it would be."

"You must be exhausted," Shannon said to Sam after Teddy's truck drove away.

"Exhausted and hungry," Sam admitted, but I don't want to go home and leave you out here alone.

"I'll be fine," she said with a grin and patted the right hip of her dusty jeans, "I'm packin', remember."

He took her hand and pulled her close. "I think I should stay," he said and glanced at the futon that she'd folded back into a couch with her blankets thrown over the back. "I can sleep in the camper," he said as he bent and kissed her, "if you want me to."

"That's the problem," Shannon mumbled between kisses. "I wouldn't want you to."

"Not a problem, then," Sam said with a broad smile. "I'll run home, grab a quick shower, some clean clothes, and pick up some food to bring back. What do you prefer pizza or pizza?"

"Pizza, I think," she said with a nervous giggle, "but I like pineapple on mine."

Sam grimaced. "Ugh, pineapple on pizza? Must be a white man thing."

"Polynesian, I think," she said.

"If you say so." He moved toward the door. "Pizza with pineapple it is."

❁

Sylvia Sweetwater stood with Nathan Dog Soldier beside his ruined Land Rover with a sour look on her wrinkled face. "This is unacceptable," Sylvia snapped. "Who does she think she is, taking pot-shots at an unsuspecting person. She should be jailed."

"I know, sweetheart," Nathan said and shrugged his burly shoulders, "but the Tribal Police can't do anything about it because the white bitch's property is technically off the reservation. Gray Wolf wrote up an official police report for the insurance, but that's as far as he could go."

"He's a worthless piece of shit," Sylvia hissed. "I don't know how he ever got elected to the position of Tribal Sheriff."

Nathan shrugged. "The traditional way," Nathan said. " Family on the Council of Elders."

"And, of course, you couldn't go to the white County police because they wouldn't do anything to a rich white woman who shot at a big, bad Indian."

"It's why I didn't bother even though one of her bullets winged Paul in the shoulder," he said as he stared at the bloody spot on his upholstery.

Sylvia shook her head. "It's criminal, but she's white, so she'll get away with it." She took Nathan's hand and rested her silver head on his shoulder. "She'll be getting put into her place soon, Chief Dog Soldier, and when the court rules in favor of the Tribe, I want to be there to see you drag the bitch off our sacred Tribal land by her blonde hair."

Nathan grinned and patted the side of Sylvia's head. "I'm looking forward to it, my sweet lady, but won't that upset your son and take money away from his business."

Sylvia shrugged. "She can buy another piece of land and pay Sam to do it all over again. Della from the bank says the bitch is loaded. She won the lottery or something when she lived down in the valley with her white husband."

"Probably left the poor fool down there to come up here to consort with red men like the white whore she is," Nathan sneered.

"She's ruining my Sam's chances of being elected Tribal Governor," Sylvia lamented and snuggled closer into Nathan. "Nobody will vote for him once they know he's sleeping with a white woman who's trespassing on our sacred land."

"And that he's helping her to build over our ancestors' bodies. It's certainly a disgraceful situation into which he's put his poor mother. I don't know how you show your face in public these days, sweet lady."

Sylvia began to sob. "The bitch is ruining everything, Nathan. I don't know what to do. My Sammy would make an ideal Governor if only he'd listen to reason and marry a suitable Native woman."

"There is still time, Sylvia. The filing deadline is still three months away. I thought about running myself," Nathan said with a sly smile the woman couldn't see, "but sadly, I'm in the same marital situation as your boy. I, too, am without a suitable Native wife at my side."

🐉

Sam woke to the shrill scream of a woman. He rolled over and reached for Shannon, but she wasn't there. He bolted upright in her folded-out futon, kicked off the tangle of blankets, and ran naked to the door. He saw Shannon standing in front of her mailbox outside the open gate. Her face was red, and she had a hand to her mouth.

Sam slid on his discarded boxers, rushed out the door, and ran down the drive to join her. "What's wrong?" he yelled in a frantic tone.

"Snake," Shannon mumbled and pointed at the securely closed mailbox.

Sam reached for the latch, and Shannon grabbed his arm and warned, "Be careful, Sam."

Sam pulled open the mailbox and jumped away with Shannon. They both bent to peek inside from a distance.

"Good lord," Sam swore and crossed the road to pick up a piece of deadfall from a cedar. He poked the branch inside the mailbox and pulled out the dead carcass of a large rattlesnake with a piece of paper tied around its neck strung through a black satin ribbon.

After poking the snake a few times to make certain it was indeed dead, Sam snatched away the note. It read: GET OFF OUR LAND OR THE NEXT SNAKE WILL BITE.

"Nathan's work?" Shannon asked, trembling as the adrenalin wore off.

Sam picked up the dead snake and flung it into the stand of cedars across the road. "It's certainly the kind of thing he'd probably do, but there are others who might have done it as well if Nathan has the Brethren worked up about you."

"Or your mother has the tribal women worked up about you."

"Both are possibilities," Sam groaned and put an arm around Shannon's waist as they walked back to the cabin.

"I think I'll start picking up my mail at the Post Office in town."

"Probably a good idea," he said and kissed her cheek.

❧ 6 ❧

October brought the first snowfall, and Shannon was happy to have a fire in the fireplace Sam had completed with the river rock and bookshelves exactly as she'd sketched them.

"This place is almost finished," Sam said as he stepped out of the bathroom wrapped in a plush cotton towel. "Now that the walls are painted, you can start hanging all that art you've been collecting."

Shannon smiled and glanced at the stack of canvasses leaning against the wall beneath the window in the living room. She and Sam had spent hours together in antique shops and secondhand stores in the area over the past month and found some great buys. Her favorite was a framed original oil on canvas of an elk bellowing in the misty morning at the foot of a pine-covered mountain. It had an artist's signature on the front she didn't recognize and a gallery tag on the back. She intended to investigate it online as soon as she got her internet and satellite TV set up.

"That's the plan as soon as all the furniture is delivered and set up," Shannon said with a grin. "The last of it should be here this afternoon."

Shannon slapped his ass as he walked by. She couldn't get enough of his tawny-skinned body. She didn't see a red man. She saw an athletically built man who spent a lot of time in the sun, who just happened to wear his jet-black hair long. Peter, her first serious boyfriend in college, and Ken had both been big compared to Sam; both were over six feet tall and over two hundred and fifty pounds, but both men were soft. They worked indoors, Peter an accountant, and Ken a middle school math and science teacher. Sam stood only an inch or two taller than Shannon's five foot eight, but his body was hard and muscular from his work outdoors, and Shannon loved it.

"The bed, I hope," Sam said with a chuckle. "I'm tired of putting up and folding out that damned couch every day."

"You're just gonna whine when you can't roll over and warm your ass with the fireplace because there's not one in the bedroom."

"That's what you're for, woman," Sam said, swatting her behind playfully, then dropping into one of the chairs at the kitchen table where a hot cup of coffee waited.

Her cell phone buzzed with a call, and Shannon glanced at the screen before answering. "It's my lawyer," she said and answered it on speaker so that Sam could hear the conversation. "Hello, this is Shannon Duncan."

"Terry Driscoll, Mrs. Duncan. I'm glad I caught you. I have some news about your suit with the Zuni." Terry Driscoll had been recommended to Shannon by a friend in Phoenix who knew several attorneys in the state and told her Driscoll had a good track record with cases like hers. He'd required a twenty-five-thousand-dollar retainer, but Shannon had written the check without batting an eye. Keeping her land and home was important to her, and Shannon would spend whatever it took to beat this ridiculous spiteful suit the Tribe had filed.

"What's the word?" she asked as she picked up her cup of coffee and took a sip.

"As I told you in my office when you came in," Driscoll said, "I think this is a frivolous and unfounded suit by the Tribe to acquire your land adjacent to the reservation and nothing more."

Shannon glanced up at Sam and saw him frowning. He'd suggested more than once that she should simply sign the land over to the Zuni and spend the money she was spending on legal fees to buy other property in the area. She'd refused to consider it, saying it had become a matter of principle now, and she refused to be bullied into giving up her property by anyone, especially Nathan Dog Soldier and his Brethren goons.

She'd spent years dreaming and planning for her retirement on this piece of private heaven. Granted, she'd planned to be spending that retirement with Ken, but that was another matter. This was her land, and nobody was going to force her off for no good reason.

"I couldn't agree more, Mr. Driscoll," Shannon sighed and smiled weakly across the table at Sam, "but how are we going to proceed from here?"

"As the Tribe claims that your property is an ancient Zuni burial ground, we will outflank them and prove that it is not."

Sam cleared his throat. "And just how do you plan to do that, Mr. Driscoll?"

"And who, may I ask, is that?" Driscoll asked. "This is a privileged attorney/client conversation."

"It's my friend, Sam Sweetwater," Shannon said, furrowing her brow and frowning at Sam.

"Any relation to that obnoxious shrew Sylvia Sweetwater, who is continually flooding the County court with frivolous suits regarding the Zuni Tribe?"

Sam chuckled. "My very own obnoxious mother, Mr. Driscoll."

Shannon heard the attorney sigh on the other end of the phone. "Do you think it wise to have this man privy to our private conversation in this matter, Mrs. Duncan? He could be passing on our strategy to that mother of his and Mr. Tyler."

"I do," Shannon said and grinned uneasily at Sam, who continued to frown. "Now, please tell me what you have in mind to disprove the Zuni claim to my property."

"Well," Driscoll said and coughed, "I've contacted the archeology department at Arizona State University, and they are going to send out a team of student archeologists with a professor and ground-penetrating radar equipment to go over every inch of your property. If there are bodies buried there, they will find them." He cleared his throat again, and Shannon waited for the other shoe to drop. "But it won't be without some expense on your part. The University requires a hundred thousand dollars in advance as a security deposit on their equipment and services."

"Not a problem," Shannon said, and she watched Sam roll his eyes and twirl his finger over his temple, indicating he thought she was crazy. "I'll bring you a check on Monday to cover it, Mr. Driscoll."

"They also expect you to secure lodging for the team while they are here and cover their meals."

"Done," Shannon said. "Let me know how many rooms they'll need and how many people will be eating, and I'll take care of it."

"I must say," Driscoll said, "that I'm impressed with your determination in this, Mrs. Duncan, and I'm confident we'll come out on top in this matter."

"It's my home," she said, "and I'll do whatever it takes to keep it. Thank you for your persistence, Mr. Driscoll. I'll see you on Monday." Shannon disconnected and put the phone on the round, white pedestal table she'd purchased along with chairs for the kitchen.

Sam snorted. "The only thing that old crook is confident of is parting you from your money, Mrs. Duncan." Sam chuckled and emptied his cup. "You know you could buy a nicer piece of land and build a great custom cabin for that kind of money," Sam scolded. "Getting the better of Sylvia and Nathan isn't really worth all that money."

"It's worth it to me," Shannon said and went to the door to peek out. "I think the new furniture is here," she said with excitement in her voice and clapped her hands.

"It's your money," Sam said, coming up behind her and wrapping his arms around her waist, "I just hope you know what you're doing."

"I'm fighting for my home," she said as he planted a kiss on the back of her head. "I can afford it."

"You never said where you got all this money you part with so easily," he said as he slipped on his jeans and a T-shirt.

"Is it important?" Shannon asked with a nervous grin. Sam had never asked her about her money before.

Teddy and Micah drove in behind the furniture truck and parked, distracting Sam from her question. "Did you guys show up just to help unload Shannon's furniture?" Sam called in a cheerful tone.

Micah took a stringer of fish out of the cooler in the back of his pickup truck and smiled, "Not on your life, boss," he said. "This is our day off. We brought Shannon some fish for her supper. She told me how much she liked to fish, and the crappie were biting out at the lake today."

They walked into the house, and Shannon propped the doors open so the men from the store could bring in the furniture.

"It's about time you got some good chairs for a man to sit on," Teddy said with a smile as he dropped into one of the hard wooden chairs at the table.

"You're not supposed to be sitting on your ass while you're here," Sam said with a good-natured smile, "you're supposed to be on your feet working."

Shannon took the stringer of fish from Micah with a broad smile on her face. "Are all of these for me?" She then noticed the tiny split on his lip with swelling. "What happened? Did one of those fish put up a fight getting it into the boat?"

Teddy gave his cousin a quick glance before turning to Sam. "Paul and a couple of his boys were at the lake when we got there," he said, "and got mouthy about Shannon and us working for her."

Sam rolled his eyes. "I'm sure they did, but you didn't need to engage them."

"They weren't very nice about what they were saying," Micah said.

Teddy snorted. "They were downright nasty," he said with a grin, "and Paul was sporting a big bandage on his shoulder with a bullet wound beneath it, so he was especially nasty."

Shannon giggled. "I'm glad to know I got one of the mouthy bastards."

Teddy chuckled. "They were much more pissed about the damage you did to big chief Nathan's fancy damned truck," he said.

"I saw that," Sam said with a grin. "He's still waiting for the dealership to get him new glass for the damned thing."

"I'm just sorry I didn't wing the big chief too," Shannon said with a grin. "I'm sorry they took it out on you, though, Micah."

Micah grinned. "You said you liked crappies," he said as he dropped the stringer into the deep white enameled sink, "so we strung those for you. Teddy and me like bass, so we kept those for our wives to fry up."

"Thanks," Shannon said and gave Micah's cheek a quick peck, "I haven't had fresh fish in quite a while."

"Hey, what about me?" Teddy said, offering his cheek to Shannon. "I'm the one who caught most of those."

Shannon ran water over the fish, went to the table, and kissed Teddy's cheek as well. "Thank you, Teddy. I really appreciate them and you boys standing up for my honor with the Brethren."

Sam grabbed Shannon's wrist and pulled her away from his blushing employee. He caught her up in his strong arms and planted a kiss on her lips. "I'm the only man you're supposed to be kissing around here."

Shannon pushed away with a smile. "Maybe when you get all those fish cleaned."

Sam's eyes went wide. "Indian men don't clean fish," he exclaimed. "the women do that."

"I'm a white woman in case you hadn't noticed, Mr. Sweetwater, and we don't clean fish when there's a man around to do it."

Micah and Teddy broke up laughing as Shannon showed the delivery men where she wanted them to place the brown leather club chairs they carried in.

After an early supper of fish, fried potatoes, slaw, and cornbread, Shannon and Sam set about arranging the new furniture, hanging curtains, and making the new queen size bed. Shannon had painted the bedroom walls a pale blue-green and the trim around the doors and window a contrasting bright white. The lace bed skirt matched the curtains on the window and French doors that led out to the covered flagstone patio. She anticipated spending many evenings in the comfortable patio furniture around the fire pit or in the swing with her laptop as she typed up Western romances.

"This room looks way too girlie for me," Sam said as he stood at the door, watching Shannon tie the creamy lace curtains back from the patio doors with wide, pink satin ribbons. Canvasses painted with floral bouquets, framed in heavy antique brass frames waited to be hung on the walls, and lamps with ornate glass shades rested on the nightstands beside the queen-size brass bed.

"I was going for that Victorian bordello look, actually," Shannon said with an impish grin.

Chuckling, Sam grabbed Shannon by the waist and flung her, giggling onto the bed she'd just dressed in a frilly pink and green pastel comforter with coordinating pillow shams.

"I don't know if I'll be able to perform in a room with all this lace and pink," he sighed between passionate kisses.

Shannon reached down, ran her hand over the hard bulge in his jeans, and smiled into his brown eyes the shade of sweet maple syrup. "I think you'll do just fine."

Sam sighed as a shiver of desire ran through his body with her touch. "You make me feel like no other woman ever has, Shannon. You make me feel like a young buck again who still has his whole life ahead of him."

"You do," she whispered as she ran her fingers through his silky, black hair, "you still have lots of years ahead of you. How old is your mother?"

"Seventy-two," he said uneasily and rolled onto his back.

"And your father? How old is he?"

Sam sighed. "I have no idea. Some guy she met at a party knocked Sylvia up with me when she was fourteen. I never knew him, and Sylvia can't--or won't tell me anything about him--not even his name--if she even remembers what it was. She just said he was Zuni, and that should be enough to satisfy me. He could be dead already for all I know."

"I'm sorry," Shannon said, "it's none of my business, and I shouldn't have brought it up."

"Don't be ridiculous," he said. "I'm the guy sharing your bed. You have every right to ask me questions. What about your parents? I don't think I've ever heard you talk about them."

"We had contentious relationships," Shannon sighed, "but they're both dead now. My father died in his fifties after what the authorities called a hunting accident, but I'm pretty sure he shot himself. He was a self-absorbed ass, and my mother had just divorced him--again." Shannon didn't like talking about her parents. "My mother died of breast cancer when she was sixty-five."

Sam ran a hand over her left breast with a look of concern on his face. "You get the test for that?"

"Every year," she said. "And I had the DNA test done for the genetic markers for the predisposition to breast cancer, but I don't have them. My mother was a heavy smoker for most of her life, and she liked her Kahlua and Creams a little too much."

"Oh," he said and was quiet for a minute before asking, "They the ones who left you all the cash?"

The money thing again? Really? Shannon guessed she should go ahead and tell him. It wasn't that big a deal.

Shannon rose on her elbow and stared down at Sam, who stared up at the ceiling, avoiding her eyes. "I won it in the damned lottery. Ok?"

"How much?"

"Fifteen million after they took the taxes out and the reduction because I wouldn't do the long-term pay-out thing."

"Wow," Sam said with a whistle. "You really are rich."

"I suppose," she sighed.

"How much of that did your husband end up with?"

Shannon snorted. "Not one damned dime after I gave him the hundred grand to cover this place."

"He didn't fight you for any of it in the divorce?"

"Not yet," Shannon sighed, "but he probably will once he thinks about it for a while and gets his ear chewed on by his significant other who wants them to retire to a beach house in San Felipe."

Sam rolled over to stare at her. "I'm sorry, Shannon. I didn't know. You never said what happened between the two of you."

7

Shannon stood in her kitchen, loading the dishwasher, when a loud crash outside caused her to drop the plate she had in her hand.

She rushed to the table beside the door, pulled out her gun, and walked out onto the patio. An old pickup with a heavy metal grill welded to the front pushed at the blocks, making up the raised beds around the perimeter of the patio. The huge vehicle knocked them to the ground to her dismay and crushed them beneath its wide tires as the driver laughed maniacally behind the wheel.

Shannon glanced at the drive and saw her gate had been rammed open and now lay crushed and mangled after the massive rig had run over it. The passenger door opened, and Nathan Dog Soldier slid out with a smirk on his broad, tawny face. "You're one hard-headed white woman, Mrs. Duncan. I'd have thought you'd have been long gone from here by now, but it looks like it's going to take some more persuading on the part of the Brethren to make that happen."

Shannon raised the shiny 357 and aimed it at the man. "And I'd have thought you'd know better than to come back for more of what I gave you the last time, Mr. Tyler," she said, trying to sound fierce, though her heart pounded in her chest as three more men jumped from the truck, eying her with what Shannon thought was malicious intent.

This situation could get ugly for her fast.

"We should fuck this bitch to death like the warriors in the old stories did to the white invaders' women," a man who resembled a UFC wrestler said as he took a step toward Shannon.

Yep, very ugly.

She moved the gun and pointed it at the big man's forehead, "And how many of those brave warriors of yours took a slug between their eyes before they ever got the chance to dip their wicks in white pussy, I wonder?" Shannon hissed as she cocked the 357 and tried her best to hold it steady in her trembling hand.

"Now, now there's no need to be crude, Mrs. Duncan," Nathan sneered as he stepped between the man and Shannon, "we just came by to bring you this," he said and held out a folded piece of white paper with typing on it.

"What's that?" she asked without taking her eyes off the men or lowering her weapon.

"It's the notice of your court date and the bill you owe me for the work the Brethren have done on this land as we discussed at our last meeting here," Nathan said calmly. "I doubt your fancy lawyer has his shit together yet, and when the judge awards this land to our Tribe, I'm going to be the one leading the Brethren here to burn this place to the ground." He let the paper fall to the sandstone patio. "And if you're still here, we'll burn you along with it."

"Aw, Chief," the big man whined as he stared at Shannon, "I thought we were gonna do this bitch. Why should Sam be the only one getting a taste of what's between her long, white legs?"

Nathan winked at Shannon. "Be my guest," he said as he turned back toward the truck, "if you can pry that cannon out of her hands before she takes your head off with it."

Nathan stepped toward the truck. The big Native man grinned down at Shannon and licked his lips, but before he could take a step in her direction, Shannon squeezed the trigger and fired a shot above his head. His eyes went wide in surprise as the bullet shattered the passenger side door's window, and Nathan dove into the floorboard as all the other men dove inside the idling truck. The driver wheeled it around, throwing dust as he sped away. He glared and threw Shannon the finger, and she fired again, putting a hole in the tailgate of the retreating pickup.

She cringed as the truck ran over the gate again on its way out onto the dusty, rutted road. Her heart still thrumming in her chest, Shannon went inside to find her phone. Tears streamed down her face as she punched in Sam's number and waited for him to answer.

"Hey, baby," he said cheerfully. "What's up?"

Shannon gulped air before speaking. "I just had another visit from Nathan and some of his Brethren," she sobbed.

"What?" he hissed. "I'm gonna kill that son-of-a-bitch. Did they touch you? I'll kill them all if they did anything to hurt you."

Shannon exhaled a long sigh as she took control of her breathing and calmed herself. "No, I'm fine. I had my gun in my hand and sent them packing like the last time," she said, "but they were in some monster truck and tore down my gate and the stone garden beds you guys built for me." Shannon sobbed as she stared out at the mess of broken blocks and scattered black garden soil. "I'm going to need a new gate. This one is completely trashed."

"Son-of-a-bitch," Sam breathed. "Call the County Sheriff and get someone out there to take a report," he told her. "I'm in the middle of something here with my mother, but I'll be over as soon as I can get away."

Shannon's heart sank. She needed Sam to put his arms around her now more than anything she could think of. What if some of Nathan's goons decided to come back and cause more trouble?

"Do you hear me, Shan?" Sam asked when she didn't reply. "I said, call the sheriff, and I'll be there as soon as I can get away."

"Yes, I heard," Shannon sighed. "I'll call the sheriff and make a report."

"You sure you're all right?" he asked, and Shannon could hear the concern in his voice.

Shannon stepped out onto the patio, and tears slid down her face as she took in the mess around her. The patio had been so beautiful, and she'd been looking forward to filling the beds with tomatoes, peppers, cucumbers, and squash.

"I'm fine," she said as she bent to pick up the paper Nathan had dropped. "I'll call the sheriff, and I'll see you when I see you." Shannon dialed the County Sheriff's office, and the dispatcher said she would send a deputy. While she waited, she snapped pictures of the destruction with her phone and sent them in a text to Sam.

Half an hour later, a deputy in a county vehicle stopped at the mangled gate and walked up to the cabin. He took a report from her and used his phone to take pictures as well.

"You know who it was that did this, ma'am?" the deputy, a tall white man in his mid-forties, asked as Shannon poured them coffee in the cabin, where she'd invited him to sit out of the cold afternoon air.

"Nathan Tyler--or Dog Soldier," Shannon said. "I'm not sure what his legal name is, but his goons from the reservation call him Chief Dog Soldier. He wasn't driving the truck, but he was giving the orders." Shannon described the truck and the Native men with Nathan, though she hadn't heard their names. He asked to see her gun and took down the serial number to check her registration.

"I should take this," he said," until I can clear it, but I won't because you might need it for your protection."

"Thank you, Officer," Shannon said. "I wouldn't feel safe out here alone should those Brethren in their monster truck decide to make another visit."

The deputy rolled his eyes. "I know the truck," he said, "and I know who you're talking about. They're a bunch of trouble-makers." He took a deep breath as he filled out his report. "They all live over on the rez, though, so we'll have to get the Tribal Police involved in this, and that's a pain in itself."

"I understand," Shannon said as she picked up the paper Nathan had left and studied it. "I'm involved in a lawsuit with the Tribe over my property here, and that's what this harassment is all about."

"I heard," the deputy said sympathetically, and his words lost their professional tone the longer he spoke. "They've got land aplenty over on that reservation, and they don't none of 'em take care of what they got." He stared around the neat cabin with its new furniture and appliances. "This here's a real nice place, ma'am, and I'd burn it to the ground before I'd turn it over to one of them thievin' redskins to move into."

Shannon huffed lightly. "Everyone seems to want to burn my house down today."

"I'm sorry, ma'am," he said, "I just meant I wouldn't give up a nice place like this without a fight."

"I'm not," she said. "I have an attorney, and I'm fighting it in court."

The deputy stood. "That's good," he said with a smile. "I'll get this report typed up, and you can pick up a copy of it for your insurance in the next day or two. And thanks for the coffee."

"You're very welcome," Shannon said again as she walked the man out.

"You want me to help you prop that gate back up and secure it with some chain?"

"I have someone coming out in a while," she said, "but thanks for the offer."

Sam stormed into the office where his mother sat at her computer, typed invoices for the week, and wrote checks.

"You're going to need more money from your white strumpet soon, Sammy," Sylvia said with a sneer. "Most of what she gave you is used up in time and labor paid to Teddy and Micah." She grinned up at Sam from the desk. "And I haven't factored in the hours you've spent in her bed. If I had, it would have been used up weeks ago."

Sam clenched his fists as his cheeks flushed with anger. "Give it a rest, Sylvia. I'm not in the mood."

"Why? Was that the white tramp calling for your services already?"

"It was Shannon," Sam bellowed, "calling to tell me that Nathan and some of his idiot Brethren boys off the reservation just knocked down her gate and trashed stuff around her patio with their damned truck." His blood boiled when he saw the smile spread across his mother's face. "And you're one to be calling someone a tramp, Mother."

Sylvia's breath caught in her throat, and the smile disappeared. "And just what is that supposed to mean?"

"Shannon wasn't spreading her legs and getting knocked up by a stranger at fourteen," he said. "Take that however you like it, Mother, but in my book, that makes you the tramp and not Shannon."

Sylvia jumped to her feet, turned, and slapped her son's face. "At least I respected myself and my people enough to give myself to a Native man and not a white ... and I could have. I was never without offers from the white bastards in town."

Sam rubbed at his throbbing temple. "Who is my father? I'd like to know." He glowered at his scowling mother. "Or didn't you bother getting his name before you dropped your pants and spread your legs?"

He saw tears brim in his mother's watery brown eyes and almost felt sorry for her, but they'd had this argument before, and Sam didn't want to back off again. He had a right to know the other half of his lineage.

"The white men were just beginning to send young men to their war in Vietnam," Sylvia said as she returned to her office chair, "and Native men along with the Blacks were the first to be seized up in their draft. The party that night was for those being shipped away overseas." Sam watched her brush a tear from her cheek and take a cleansing breath.

"His name was Samuel Broken Feather. He was my first and only love, Sammy. He was nineteen, and he never came home from that white man's war," she sobbed. "They told his mother he was missing in action and probably a prisoner, but he never returned to his family. Not even when all the other prisoners were returned to their families alive, and they never got a body to bury either." Tears ran from Sylvia's eyes, and Sam wanted to hug her.

Sam's mouth fell open in surprise. "Broken Feather as in Melody Broken Feather who spat on me in school and called me filth because I was the bastard of an unnamed father?"

Sylvia nodded without taking her eyes off the computer screen. "The daughter of Samuel's younger brother, Evan, who spent most of his miserable life in prison for stealing cars to support his drug habit." She shook her head. "That boy was always in trouble for something, and his daughter had no right to disparage you."

Sam had had a crush on the pretty, petite girl all through

school and could never understand her dislike of him. "She was my cousin? Did her family know about me?"

Sylvia snorted. "They knew," she said. "Samuel wrote and told them after I wrote and told him I was expecting, but they were afraid I'd make a claim to the Army for benefits, and they didn't want to share any of it with you or me."

Sam shook his head. "And you rant about the greed of the white man." He walked out of the office toward the kitchen. "Those people were my blood, and they didn't want to share the few hundred dollars the Army might have paid a dependent child. I can't believe you sometimes, Mother. They were the greedy ones and not Shannon."

"Amanda recognized you as her grandson before she died," Sylvia said, "but the rest of her children refused to recognize you, though you're the spitting image of your father."

Sylvia opened the desk drawer, withdrew a ragged, sepia photo taken with a Polaroid camera, and handed it to Sam. In the faded photo, the sweaty boy, his long, disheveled hair hanging from a battered cowboy hat and his boots dusty and scuffed, could have been Sam as a teenager.

"This is my father?" Sam asked, staring at the precious photo in his hands

"At the reservation rodeo," Sylvia said with pride, "the summer before he got his draft notice. He'd just taken first place in the calf roping event."

"Why would you never tell me about him or show me this picture? I don't understand, Mother."

"It," she said with a sob, "and you were all that I had left of him, and I wanted to keep it to myself."

Sylvia's phone chimed with a text, and she glanced away from Sam to read it. She looked back up at her son with a broad smile on her wrinkled face. "That was from the Pueblo in New Mexico. They need us to travel there for you to file the paperwork to run for Tribal Governor." Sylvia got to her feet and wrapped an arm around her son. "I've arranged a dinner for a few women from the Tribe at the restaurant in the casino and us. You should show up at the Pueblo with a suitable bride-to-be on your arm, not some white tramp with a fat bank account as her only redeeming quality."

"We're done here, Mother," Sam said in an irritated tone. "I told you before that I'm not running for Tribal Governor, and I'm not going to marry a Native woman just to accomplish that."

"Your father wanted to be Tribal Governor someday," she sighed. "And he would have been if he'd come back from that white man's war. We would have been the Zuni First Family and lived in the Pueblo in New Mexico."

"But he didn't come back, Mother, and he didn't marry you or give me his damned name." Sam glared down at his mother. "I took you out of that shabby shack we lived in on the reservation and put you in this nice house." He motioned around the room. "Isn't that enough for you, Sylvia?"

He saw her wince when he used her name rather than calling her Mother. Sam knew it pissed her off, and he did it when she irritated him, which was most of the time since he'd reached adulthood. Why couldn't she let him live his life the way he saw fit? Perhaps the photo of the boy he held in his hand was the reason.

"I'm not that boy, Mother, and you can't live the life you dreamed of with him vicariously through me."

Sam shoved the Polaroid of Samuel Broken Feather into his back pocket and stormed out of the house with Sylvia still reaching out for her precious photo. He got into his truck and headed toward Shannon's. The sun would be setting soon, and Sam wanted his truck in Shannon's driveway before then.

Shannon rushed into his arms when he got out of his truck at the ruined gate. He held her as she sobbed into his shoulder and her anguished weeping made him want to wring Nathan Tyler's neck.

"I'm so sorry, baby," Sam said and kissed the top of her head, "but me and the boys will have this put back together as good as new before you know it."

"I'm sorry you guys have to do all this work all over again," she said, choking on her words, "but I can't give up. I refuse to let that son-of-a-bitch run me off my land. I called Mr. Driscoll, and he said he got a copy of the notice from the court and made another call to the University." She stepped back, took a deep breath, and wiped her eyes with the back of her hand. "He said the archeologists would be here next week with their radar equipment, and then this will all be over with."

Sam kissed her again and smiled. "That would be good, but let's get this poor gate lifted off the ground and throw some chains around it, so no more rodents get in overnight."

❦ 8 ❧

Shannon stood in the small Post Office, waiting to get to her box when a headline and photo on the front of the Tribal Newspaper caught her eye.

SWEETWATER ANNOUNCES HIS RUN FOR TRIBAL GOVERNOR AND UPCOMING NUPTIALS.

Since the incident with the dead rattler in her mailbox, Shannon had been picking up her mail from one of the local Post Office's rented boxes. She folded the paper in her hand as she moved forward, put the brass key into the lock, and opened the door to extract the mail stuffed inside. She only drove into town once a week, so the grocery flyers delivered on Tuesdays filled the box, though she'd repeatedly requested they not be put into her box.

Today another official-looking envelope was added to the mix, and Shannon pulled it out carefully, suspecting it to be something from Mr. Driscoll regarding the lawsuit. A Phoenix attorney's name filled the top left corner of the manila envelope, but Shannon didn't recognize it. She waited until she got back to her Jeep to open it and saw that the envelope contained divorce papers from Ken.

"Well, I knew these were coming," she mumbled to herself as she scanned the stapled papers. Her mouth fell open when she read Ken was suing her for her abandonment of the marriage and wanted half her assets, including the improved property she inhabited.

"I don't think so, asshole," Shannon hissed and threw the papers onto the passenger seat along with the folded newspaper. She would attend to that later. "I'll fight you and the whole Zuni Tribe if I have to, but nobody is getting my home and land, especially not you and your sweetheart Dale Eubanks," Shannon said out loud.

Shannon dialed Ken's number and was surprised when another male voice answered. "I'd like to speak with Ken, please."

"Who is this?" the man demanded.

"This is his wife," Shannon sneered, knowing the man had to be Dale Eubanks.

"Kenny has nothing to say to you, bitch," Dale snarled into the phone. "Do you have any idea how you humiliated him by leaving him penniless the way you did?"

"Like I was humiliated by you in my own home that night, Dale, when you demanded my husband and then tried to choke me out and take my money?" Shannon demanded. "And I left the bastard with a hundred grand in cash, Dale. You can hardly call that penniless."

"It was Kenny's money too, bitch, and he's gonna get his fair share when he sues you for divorce."

"We'll see about that, Dale. Tell Ken I got his attorney's papers, and I'm taking them to my attorney now. He can expect my reply in the very near future," Shannon snarled before disconnecting.

Shannon backed out of the parking lot, throwing gravel in her wake, and drove to Mr. Driscoll's office. She marched inside with the divorce papers in her hand, and his secretary took Shannon into Driscoll's small but well-appointed office without asking her if she had an appointment.

"What can I do for you today, Mrs. Duncan?" he asked with a raised brow when he saw the stern look on Shannon's face. "The team from the University will be here the day after tomorrow. Is there something we need to talk about as far as they are concerned?"

"No," she said and handed Driscoll the papers from the attorney in Phoenix, "it's that other matter I told you might come up soon."

"Oh, I see," he said as he scanned the papers.

Driscoll glanced up at Shannon above the rim of his thick glasses with a furrowed brow. "You told me you paid your husband for his title to the property, did you not?"

"I left him with a hundred thousand in hundred dollar bills," Shannon sighed, "but I didn't get a bill of sale or anything like that. If that's what you mean. I was a little distraught at the time and just wanted to get the hell out of that house."

Driscoll frowned, and Shannon felt as though she were sitting in front of her high school principal. "I assume Mr. Duncan and his attorney are unaware of your lawsuit with the Zuni, concerning your property then."

Shannon shook her head. "I've had no contact with Ken since I left that night. I don't even know how he got my mailing address here."

Driscoll smiled as he scribbled notes on a yellow legal pad. "And this claim of abandoning your marriage?"

"Only after his boyfriend told me they were making plans together for a beach house in Mexico and then tried to strangle me and take my checkbook," Shannon said as she crossed and uncrossed her legs nervously in the leather chair.

Abandoned, indeed! She wasn't the one who screwed up this marriage, and she hadn't abandoned anything. She'd left a husband who was cheating on her. In all their years together, she'd never looked at another man. How could he claim she'd abandoned their marriage?

"I see, and the other assets referred to here? You came into your windfall while still in the marriage, I assume?"

"On the same day, I found out a man in my marriage bed had replaced me," Shannon said uneasily as her cheeks burned with embarrassment and shame.

"I think we'll be able to shut this whole thing down before it gets out of hand," Driscoll said with a confident grin. "First, I'll send his attorney an overview of your suit with the Zuni, including a detailed list of my accumulated billable hours, the money you've put on deposit with the University, and their lodging expenses." Driscoll took a deep breath. "I will then demand your husband sign a quitclaim deed for the property over to you or a contract, guaranteeing he pays his half of all the expenses of the case and his acceptance of the possibility the land might be lost should the case not go our way." Driscoll smiled and shrugged. "He will be forced to either play or pay."

Shannon smiled. "And what about the other stuff?"

"Unfortunately," the attorney sighed, "Arizona is a community property state, so you will probably have to make him some sort of monetary offer, if not half your winnings."

"How much?" Shannon asked. "I don't mind giving him some of the money if we can make this mess go away. There's more than enough for me to live well on for the rest of my life, but," she hesitated, "but I hate funding the lifestyle of that little weasel, Dale Eubanks."

Driscoll raised his hands in a defensive posture. "I understand, perfectly, Mrs. Duncan. Does your husband know how much lottery money you won?" There was that accusatory tone again.

Shannon furrowed her brow. "Yes, but in all the years of

our marriage, we've always kept our money separate and in different banks."

Driscoll shrugged as he continued to make notes on the yellow pad. "We'll make a fractional offer to your husband and see what happens." Driscoll glanced up over the rim of his glasses again. "I'll also demand a speedy court date and set up depositions with all of his co-workers at the school where he is employed to see what they know about his extramarital relationship with this Eubanks man."

Shannon's eyes went wide. "Ken wouldn't have let it be known around the school that he had a homosexual relationship."

Driscoll smiled slyly. "Exactly!"

"Oh," Shannon said, understanding the attorney's strategy of embarrassing Ken into dropping his ridiculous demands in the divorce. "I'll leave it in your capable hands, then, Mr. Driscoll. Do you need another retainer check to handle the divorce?"

Driscoll smiled as he stood. "I think we're good for now, Mrs. Duncan."

Shannon shook the attorney's soft, smooth hand and left the office.

Sam's going to be surprised about that one.

In the car, Sam's face smiled up at her from the passenger seat, and Shannon picked up the Tribal Newspaper and read the lengthy article about how Sam Sweetwater, local business owner and Tribal dignitary, had filed his intent with the Zuni Pueblo in New Mexico to run for Tribal Governor of the Zuni people. It also mentioned how Sam intended to marry before taking up the mantle of Tribal Governor, though it mentioned no name of the prospective bride.

On the following page, Shannon saw the photo of a beautiful Native woman with the name Karla Black Fox Sweetwater 1968-1998 printed below it, along with the story about how she'd been a teacher at the reservation's elementary school, who'd raised herself out of the poverty of the reservation and attended college, but returned to educate the children, and was killed in an accident with a drunken white woman who was never prosecuted for the incident.

How horrible for Sam to have to see this in the paper after all this time. And she had been such a pretty woman.

Shannon's heart skipped a beat when she read further where it said Mr. Sweetwater was on the search for a suitable replacement for his poor dead wife, a Native woman who could stand by his side as a proper First Lady of the Zuni People.

Shannon was sure that came straight from the mouth of Sylvia. She was probably in her office, taking applications as Shannon sat here reading.

۞

Sam sat in the noisy bar with the Tribal Newspaper spread open on the table. He'd been receiving congratulations since he walked into the room with Teddy and Micah for a quick burger.

"I had no idea you planned to run, boss," Micah said after the waitress brought a pitcher of beet to their table and told them it was on the house.

"I don't," Sam snapped as he shoved the paper aside. "This is all Sylvia's doing, not mine. I've got no interest in politics, and you guys know that better than anyone."

"If you're serious about that wife thing," the pretty Native waitress dressed in skin-tight jeans and a revealing T-shirt said, batting her thick, dark lashes at Sam as she filled their glasses with Bud, "both me and my mom are available, 'cause you'd probably be more my mom's age than mine."

Teddy rolled his eyes and laughed. "Go on, Rita. Sam's not interested in lounge lizard trash like you or your whiskey guzzling mother." The girl walked away with an indignant scowl on her face. "Guess you're gonna have to expect more of that, Boss," Teddy said with a grin. "I wonder what Miss Shannon's gonna think?"

Sam's face darkened. "Shannon," he sighed and stared from his friends to the crowd in the bar. "She'd have no reason to pick up one of these Tribal rags."

Micah snorted as he picked up the paper with Sam's face smiling on the front page. They'd used a close-up taken from his wedding photos with Karla, and the smile on his twenty-year younger face blinded Sam. It had been one of the happiest days, and seeing the photo made him want to cry. "Not unless she was in a checkout line and saw your mug smiling out at her with the headline, saying you're running for governor and looking for a Zuni wife," Micah said. "Then she might be tempted to pick one up."

"This is all Sylvia's doing," Sam hissed and slammed his palm on the top of the table, causing beer to slosh out of the pint tumblers. "She must have gone to the Pueblo last week with Nathan and filed the paperwork I never filled out. She can forge my signature easily enough. Then she gave this ridiculous story to the paper."

"She's your mother," Teddy said with a shrug of his broad shoulders, "She just wants what's best for you, Sam."

"She wants to live my life like it's the one she couldn't have with the man who fathered me." Micah and Teddy stared at him when he got to his feet and tossed two twenties on the table. "I gotta go try to explain all of this bullshit to Shannon. You guys can handle finishing up today, right?"

"Yeah, sure, boss," Teddy said. "We can handle it. Go do what you gotta do."

The loud ringing and cartoon music of slot machines, along with the voices of laughing people, made it difficult for Sylvia to hear as she sat with Nathan at the central bar in the casino, sipping a cold beer. She hadn't wanted to go out today, but Nathan had insisted, so she'd dressed in her best wool suit, adorned herself from her collection of Native jewelry, and joined Nathan for an early dinner and drinks at the busy casino built on reservation property. Tribe members received handsome checks each month as shareholders, and Sylvia smiled. It did her heart good to see all the white fools sliding bills into the noisy machines. What better revenge could it be for the Natives against the whites who'd trapped them on these reservations over a hundred years ago than to separate them from their money? The fools came and gave it willingly, and it all went back into the pockets of the Native families on the reservation.

"Do you think he's seen the paper yet?" Nathan asked as he punched the buttons to hold the cards on the video poker machine set into the bar top.

She only wished so many of her own people didn't give it all back every month.

Sylvia smiled. "I'm sure he has. I've been getting calls from eligible women all morning."

Nathan chuckled. "I'd give my left ball to have seen his face and that of his white bitch." He patted Sylvia's hand. "I'm sure she'll throw his ass out now, Syl." He punched more buttons and watched the cards change on the screen. "Shame, though. We could have used some of that cash of hers. If Sam married her," Nathan said with a brow cocked, "and the bitch met with an accident, all that money would be his."

He winked at the silver-haired woman who must have been a real beauty in her day. Nathan preferred younger women, but this one had proven to be a cash cow and easy to manipulate with sweet words to balm her massive ego. He'd continue to carry on with her for as long as her money held up, but her son would likely become more of a problem than it was worth soon.

"I don't care about her damned money," Sylvia hissed as she pulled her hand away from Nathan's. "She's white ... and she's wrong for my Sammy. He needs a good Native woman at his side."

"Her damned money is paying our bills, darling lady," Nathan said with a chuckle. "You're the only good Native woman Sam needs at his side, Sylvia." Nathan patted the woman's hand. "Let him milk this white cow for as long as it lasts."

"But he needs a Native wife at his side to be elected governor, Nathan," Sylvia said. "I can't let him end up with that white bitch who is going to ruin his chances at the governorship."

"You seem to be more interested in becoming the mother of the governor than anything else," Nathan sneered.

❦ 9 ❦

The loud squawking of her hens woke Shannon, and she bolted up in bed. The engine of a truck revved, and she heard a metallic crashing noise out front.

Now what?

The pale November sun filtered through the lace curtains as Shannon pulled them aside to peek out at her patio through the panes of the French doors. Her heart raced in her chest, and her breath caught in her throat when she saw dozens of snakes slithering across the sun-warmed sandstone pavers, trapping her inside the cabin. Shannon couldn't tell what kind of snakes they were, but she didn't intend to go out and make a closer inspection. The one in her mailbox had been a rattler, and the thought of it sent another chill up her spine.

Shannon shivered. She hated snakes about as much as she hated spiders.

The engine of a truck revved again, and Shannon's eyes flashed to the road where a truck raced away, dragging her gate along behind it, causing a whirlwind of dust to billow up in its wake. It was the same large pickup from before, and anger surged through Shannon's veins as she remembered the devastation it had wrought on her block planters the last time.

In the sky, dark clouds gathered, and Shannon remembered the forecast the night before of rain turning to sleet and possibly more snow for today. The clouds reflected her mood as she watched the snakes slithering across her patio. Didn't snakes go underground in cold weather?

Why couldn't these assholes just leave her alone? Sam needed to figure out a way to mount another gate these assholes couldn't pull down.

Shannon stirred the few glowing embers in the fireplace, added some split cedar logs, and waited for small blue flames to lick up the wood before she slipped on her warm, terry robe. Then she shoved her feet into her fleece-lined slippers and rushed to the back door, where she hesitated before yanking it open, studying the small sandstone patio for more snakes. Shannon breathed a sigh of relief when she didn't see any, but the chicken coop Sam and his crew had constructed the week before had been pulled down, and her dozen gray Barred Rock hens were scattered around the back yard, clucking in distress as they scratched in the yellowed winter grass.

Shannon exhaled another long sigh of relief when she counted the birds and saw none had been injured or trapped in the tangle of wood and chicken wire of the ruined coop.

The poor things probably won't lay for a month after this.

She went to the table, picked up her phone, and punched in Sam's number. It went directly to voice mail, and Shannon left him a frantic message about the snakes, the pickup she recognized, her chicken coop, and her gate.

Where are you, Sam? I need you.

Unable to reach Sam, Shannon called the sheriff's office next and asked them to please send out animal control to collect the snakes. She must have sounded like a nut-job because the woman on the other end of the phone spoke to as though she was talking to someone tripping on narcotics.

"How many snakes do you see, ma'am?" the woman

asked, and Shannon could hear the mirth in her voice as she continued. "Are you certain it's more than one?"

Shannon grimaced. "Did you see that Indiana Jones movie where he falls into the old temple with all the snakes?" Shannon asked in an irritated tone. She heard the woman grunt an affirmative reply. "Well, not quite that bad, but close. My patio is crawling with the damned things, and someone pulled down my chicken coop out back. My poor hens are loose out there with snakes everywhere."

"Ma'am," she heard the woman say in a reprimanding tone, "Animal Control can't help you collect your escaped chickens."

"I know that," Shannon snapped and immediately felt ashamed. "Just send someone to round up these snakes, please," Shannon said in a milder tone, frustrated with herself and the situation, "before they make meals of my hens and please send out an officer so I can get a police report of this vandalism for my insurance company." She hadn't bothered to report the last incident or file a claim and wasn't certain she would this time, but she wanted the police to know what was going on out here, even if she sounded like a crazy woman on the phone.

Why did it have to be so damned hard? She just wanted to live her life on her property in peace and quiet. She wasn't causing anybody any trouble. She wished Sam was there to wrap his strong arms around her and tell her everything was going to be all right.

Sam had spent the night at home because his mother had told him she had paperwork she needed him to attend to, but Shannon suspected the old woman wanted her son at home and out of Shannon's bed.

She didn't know if she had the strength to fight the old bitch for her home and for Sam too. Maybe if she sent him back to her, she'd leave her alone and let her live in peace.

Sylvia handed Sam a cup of coffee before returning to the stove where bacon sizzled in one of the fancy new skillets Sam had bought for her when they'd moved from the reservation into this new house. Sam glanced up at his mother with a scowl on his face as he listened to Shannon's message.

"What did you have to do with this new trouble at Shannon's, Mother?" Sam growled as he slammed the phone onto the table. "Someone's been back at her place and dumped snakes on her patio."

Sylvia chuckled as she forked bacon from the skillet and put it on a plate. "I don't know what you're talking about, Sammy, but what's that they say about Karma being a bitch?"

"You're the only bitch I see around here, Sylvia," Sam mumbled loud enough for his mother to hear and then swallowed a mouth full of hot, black coffee. "I just don't understand why you, Nathan, and his blasted Brethren can't leave her alone and let the courts deal with things? The courts will settle this thing soon enough. You don't have to keep messing with her place like that."

"She's built her garish little house on sacred land," his mother snapped, "and anyhow, she pays you to fix all the little things Nathan and the Brethren mess up, doesn't she?" Sylvia added with a shrug of her narrow, bony shoulders.

"And pays me well, Sylvia, and you know it. Her projects are keeping us fed this winter."

"Good," Sylvia said as she cracked eggs into the sizzling bacon fat, "then you'll have ample funds to use for your upcoming campaign."

Sam rolled his eyes. "What campaign? I've told you before, Mother, I have no intention of running for Governor."

Sylvia picked up a bundle of papers from the counter and tossed them onto the table in front of her son. "According to those," she said with a sly smile, "you're an official candidate for Governor of the Zuni people."

Sam grimaced as he leafed through the papers. "What's this nonsense?" he asked when he came to a list of names printed from Sylvia's printer in the office.

"It's a list of names I put together of suitable Zuni women to be your new bride and our next First Lady," she said as she set plates of eggs, bacon, and buttered toast on the table before she took her seat. "You should choose one soon, Sammy, and set a date for the wedding. The paper is expecting a call from me about an announcement."

Sam's mouth fell open as he stared at his mother in amazement. "You can't be serious, Mother. I don't even know half these women."

"That's why I'm planning a little get together at the casino and inviting all of them," Sylvia said and snapped off a piece of bacon to slide into her toothless mouth. "It will give you the opportunity to get a good look at them all and make a decision."

Sam scowled at his mother, thought for a minute, then grinned. "Set it up," he said with a shrug of his muscular shoulders, "I'm sure Shannon will enjoy a nice meal in the casino's fancy dining room ... at your expense."

"You can't bring that white bit--" Sylvia gasped and choked on the coffee she'd swallowed. "You're a wicked boy, Samuel Sweetwater."

"I come by it naturally, Mother," Sam said as he shoved his chair away from the table and stood. "I've learned from the best."

"Where are you going?" Sylvia demanded. "You haven't finished the breakfast I just cooked for you."

"I lost my appetite," Sam said and tossed the papers at his mother, "and Shannon needs me. Someone pulled down her new gate, trashed her chicken coop, and dumped burlap sacks full of snakes on her patio. She's scared shitless, and I've gotta go help."

He turned toward the door as he shoved his phone into his jeans but turned back to face Sylvia again. "And if I find out you had anything to do with this," he hissed, pointing a finger at his scowling mother, "I'll pack your scrawny, red ass up and dump you back in that falling down shack you raised me in on the reservation. Without any of the new furniture, clothes, or jewelry I bought for you, either."

Sylvia twisted one of the heavy silver rings on her finger. "You wouldn't do that to the woman who gave birth to you and raised you all alone."

"Wouldn't I?" Sam spat before turning and storming toward the door. "This shit with Shannon Duncan ends now, Mother, or you can come with me, and I'll drop you at the reservation gates so you can walk in shame back to your old hovel if it's still standing. It's where crazy old Indian bitches like you belong anyhow."

"You're an ungrateful little shit, Samuel Sweetwater," Sam heard his mother scream along with a ceramic plate shattering as he stepped outside into the damp, cool morning.

"What's up, boss?" Teddy asked, grinning at Micah, where they stood beside their truck in heavy jackets, waiting for Sam. "Domestic problems?"

"More trouble at Shannon's," Sam said as he strode to the truck.

"What now?" Micah asked.

"Snakes," Sam said and climbed inside the cab and shoved the key into the ignition.

"I hate fucking snakes," Teddy groaned.

"Where did the assholes find snakes at this time of the year?" Micah asked as he snugged his jacket. "Most are burrowed up underground already."

"You've got me," Sam said with a shrug, "but she left me a message, saying the front patio was crawling with 'em."

"I'll take my truck over there," Teddy called. "I hate fucking snakes."

Sam dialed Shannon's number. When she didn't answer, he frowned with concern and left a message, saying they were on their way. He put the truck into drive and stepped on the gas with Teddy following behind.

An Apache County Sheriff's vehicle sat in Shannon's drive when they arrived, along with a truck from Animal Control parked in front of it. Two uniformed deputies and two Animal Control officers holding plastic animal crates and snake sticks stood outside the cabin. Sam didn't see Shannon, but once he'd parked, she came racing out from the back door into his arms.

"I'm so glad you're here, Sam," she said into his hair, still damp from the shower he'd taken before his almost breakfast with Sylvia.

"I was in the shower when you called," he said with concern in his coffee-brown eyes. "Are you all right?"

"Just a little spooked by those slimy bastards," Shannon said, trembling in his arms, and nodded toward the patio.

"Rattlers?" Sam asked one of the Animal Control Officers as the man walked to his truck to deposit a plastic crate and store the pole with a hook on the end.

The thin, graying man shook his head as he slipped the crate into a cubby in the rear of the truck. "No, just some Gopher Snakes and a couple of big Kings. Scary, but they wouldn't have done any damage." He took out a cigarette and lit it. "Someone was probably raising 'em to make hatbands with to sell in the tourist shops."

"We got 'em all, ma'am," the other Animal Control Officer, a slim woman, said. "There were fifteen in all, and I don't think any got under the house." She smiled and shrugged as she put away her snake pole. "Even so, they'd keep down the mice over the winter."

Shannon snorted. "That's why I have a cat."

The two deputies joined them. "I have pictures of everything," one of them said, "and you can pick up a copy of my report in a few days at the office."

"Thank you," Shannon said. "I appreciate you coming out again."

"Wish we could do a little more," the other deputy said with a glare at Sam, Teddy, and Micah, "but with them living on the reservation, it limits our ability to do much. The Reservation Police won't help us against their own."

"Hey," Teddy snarled, "don't be givin' us the stink-eye, Deputy Dog, none of us live over on the reservation anymore. We're all hard-working, tax-paying Americans just like you."

"Sure you are, Tonto," the deputy growled as he pushed past them and went to his car, where he got in on the passenger side. Sam watched him glare at Shannon through the window. She stood beside Sam with her head on his shoulder, and he smiled at the deputy as he put his arm around her waist and pulled her close.

She probably wouldn't get such good service from the Sheriff's Department the next time she called. Whites don't like their women mixing with Natives any more than his mother liked seeing Native men with white women.

Sam shook his head. "Let's go take a look at what damage they did to your chicken coop."

"It's totally trashed," Shannon sighed. "It's gonna have to be completely rebuilt."

"That's all right," Micah said in a cheerful tone as they walked, "I saw some plans in a book that would be much better than the one we built before."

Teddy whistled when he saw the twisted wire and broken wood of the busted up coop. "Man, they sure made a mess of this." He turned his head to Shannon. "Same guys as before?"

Shannon nodded. "Same big blue pickup with the monster tires on it and metal grill."

"Malcolm Tagert from over on the reservation," Teddy

sighed. "Everyone in Apache County knows that ugly, big-ass truck and the trouble he causes with it."

"But the county mounties don't do a damned thing," Micah added as he bent to pick up one of the hens, "even though his favorite pass time is running over mailboxes."

"His grandfather is a Tribal Elder," Sam sighed, "so the Tribal Police are gonna protect him if county authorities try to come onto the reservation."

Shannon shook her head. "Isn't plowing down mailboxes a Federal Offence and the reservation under Federal Jurisdiction?"

The three men began to chuckle. "As if the Feds are gonna get involved in hunting down a guy for trashing a few mail-boxes," Teddy said with a broad smile on his burnished face.

"A crime is a crime," Shannon said with a furrow in her brow, "and if they're supposed to be putting criminals in jail, they should be doing their job."

Fat raindrops began to fall, and they all turned toward the cabin. "I don't think we're gonna be getting any work done out here today," Sam said. "Do you have any more inside projects?"

Shannon grinned and shut the door against the rain that had begun to come down in cold, silver sheets. "The bath-room still needs paint, and Home Depot delivered the tile for the kitchen backsplash yesterday."

Teddy groaned. "I hate mounting tile on walls about as much as I hate snakes."

"You can paint, then," Sam said with a smile as they crowded into the warm kitchen for some hot coffee.

❧ 10 ❧

The phone rang and startled Shannon as she sat at her table, admiring the newly grouted tile backsplash behind her kitchen sink and counters.

"Hello, sir," Shannon answered the call from her attorney. "What have you heard?" she asked, trying her best not to sound overly anxious.

"I'm afraid it's not good news, Mrs. Duncan," the attorney said in his husky voice. "They found artifacts in the northwest corner that appear to have been uncovered by the recent rains."

Shannon shivered. "What sort of artifacts?" she asked with her hand clutching her cup of coffee. "Human remains?"

"No bones," he said, "but pottery and some pieces of jewelry. The professor said they could be grave goods. He's sent them back to the university with some of the students for testing while they use the ground-penetrating radar to conduct a more thorough search of the immediate area."

This was just great. Tears filled Shannon's eyes. Grave goods usually meant a grave and a grave meant remains of some sort. That would be the end of it. Sylvia Sweetwater and the Tribe would get her land.

Shannon ran her fingers through her hair. "Should I start packing?" she asked as Sam walked in, brushing snowflakes from his fleece-lined jacket. "Your birds are safely ensconced in their new home," he said with a broad smile but put a finger to his lips when he saw her on the phone. The temperature had fallen again, and the moisture in the air had changed from rain to snow.

"Now, don't throw in the towel quite yet, Mrs. Duncan," the attorney said in a soothing voice.

"But the court date is in less than two weeks. Don't you have to give the Tribe's attorney this news?"

Sam stared at her with a raised brow and a shrug of his broad shoulders.

"I do," he replied, "but not until the professor and his people have finished their examinations and have made a scientific determination about what they've found." The attorney paused. "So, try not to worry," he said, "until we know what we're dealing with."

"I'll try," she sighed. "Thank you for calling and letting me know, Mr. Driscoll."

"Letting you know what?" Sam said after Shannon dropped the phone onto the table. "Did they find something out there? I saw a new truck pull in with more equipment, but they won't be doing any digging if this keeps up." He nodded toward the window where Shannon could see heavy snow falling.

Shannon lifted her cup to her lips and sipped the cooling liquid. "They found what might be grave goods up in the northwest corner," she said.

"Then Sylvia was right all along, and this is sacred land?" he mused as he poured coffee into a mug before joining Shannon at the table. "It's always been used for ceremonies, but I never thought it was a gravesite like she's been insisting."

"The professor sent what they found to Tempe for testing, and he and his crew are going to start ground-penetrating radar scans to look for the grave they might have come from," she said as she glanced up at the window, "but I doubt they can now."

"And if they find remains?" Sam asked, putting a comforting hand on Shannon's. "Will you give up the fight with the Tribe and move?"

"This is my land," she sighed, "my home. I've—"

"If Zuni dead are buried here, Shannon," he said, cutting her off in mid-thought, "this is sacred Tribal land and must be returned to the Zuni."

Shannon's mouth fell open at Sam's forceful words. "They don't even know what they found yet," she said, "or where it washed up from. It could be something from north of my boundary stakes."

Sam sat in silence as he pondered her words. "If that's the case," he said, "then it would have come off the reservation. I suppose that's possible."

"And if it didn't come from off reservation property?" she asked, already knowing his response.

"As I said before," Sam said, staring into her eyes, "then you'll have to return the ground to the Tribe. It's sacred if our dead are buried here." He stood, walked over to touch her shoulders. "Would you really want to live in a graveyard, Shannon?"

Shannon leaned her head back to rest on his flat abdomen. "No, I don't suppose I would."

Sam kissed the top of her head. "I'm certainly not looking forward to seeing that I told you, so grin on Sylvia's face when she hears this news."

"My lawyer says he'll inform the Tribe once the professor has all the tests done in Tempe at the university, and he has conclusive proof the items are authentic," Shannon said and sipped her coffee. "You don't have to be the one to give her the good news."

Sam returned to his chair. "Does he think there's a possibility they're not authentic?"

Shannon shrugged her shoulders. "He may have been saying that for my benefit because he knows how upset I'll be to lose this land after all I've put into it."

"There's plenty of other land to be had up here, babe," Sam said with a sympathetic smile. "I bet we can find you an even better spot than this one in no time at all."

"It wouldn't be the same, Sam," Shannon said with tears stinging her eyes, "and I don't think I could go through all the construction mess again. I was so happy to call it done except for the few little things here and there." She stared around at the freshly grouted tiles on the wall behind the big farm sink, and the tears began to stream down her face. How could she just walk away from all of this? It had been her dream come to life. How could she just start all over again from scratch? "Maybe I'll just go back down to the valley," she finally muttered.

Sam's tawny face fell, and his eyes went wide in surprise. "You mean you'd just up and leave me?"

"The valley's only a couple of hours away," she said with a sigh, "and we both have phones." She picked up her phone and ran her finger over the glass front. "If I lose this place, I'm gonna need some time to recover, and my publisher has been after me for another book, so I should work on that."

Sam shot to his feet. "If you leave, you'll never come back," he said angrily. "You'll take all that money and buy a big house with a pool in Paradise Valley or Cave Creek, and I'll never see you again."

Shannon snorted. "As if I ever wanted or needed a damned pool."

"Isn't it what all the rich bitch white women in the valley do?" he sneered. "They lounge around a pool with their rich bitch friends drinking wine and talking about the latest book of the month?"

Shannon's mouth fell open in shock. "Is that really what you think of me, Sam? You think I'm a white, rich bitch version of Sylvia in her knock-off designer clothes, silver jewelry, and big rings?" Shannon stared down at her paint-stained T-shirt and jeans. "I'm about as far from that as you'll ever find, and you know it."

"Don't bring my mother into this, Shannon," Sam growled. "She's a proud Zuni woman, and her clothes and jewelry reflect exactly that."

Shannon rolled her eyes. "Right, and don't even try to tell me she wouldn't be lounging around a pool, wearing designer bathing suits, if she could talk you into laying out the cash to build one for her in your back yard."

Sam glared at her as he put on his coat. "I'll send you a bill for the work on the chicken coop, Mrs. Duncan," he said before storming back out into the blowing snow. "Damned woman," he yelled as he slammed the door hard enough to shake the cabin and rattle the kitchen windows.

How dare she bring his mother into this. Sylvia was certainly a bitch. There was no doubt about that, and she'd made Shannon's life hell since she'd moved up here from the valley, but Shannon had no right to bad mouth her that way. She was still his mother, and he was the only one who could talk shit about her.

Sam slowed his truck when he saw Nathan and two of his goons exiting old, Doc as everyone referred to him, Silver Eagle's tourist trap on Route 180 across from the reservation. They laughed and slapped one another on the back as they hurried through the blowing snow to Nathan's repaired Land Rover, which caught Sam's attention.

The old man was a retired archeologist and silversmith who'd opened his little adobe building after his retirement from the University of Arizona some years ago to sell petrified wood, silver jewelry, and reproduction Zuni pottery to the passing tourists. His curiosity getting the better of him, Sam turned around and pulled his truck into the gravel lot lined with the petrified stumps of long-dead trees.

Sam was shocked to see the glass cases shattered and silver pieces were strewn across the polished wood floor inside the building. "Doc?" Sam called out as he crunched broken glass beneath his boots. "You here, Doc?"

"I'm here," came a weak groan from behind the shattered jewelry case, and Sam rushed around to find the old man sprawled on the floor with blood dripping from his nose and his long white braids cut from his head.

"Doc?" Sam gasped as he kneeled at the old man's side. "What the hell happened here, Doc? Was it Nathan Tyler and his band of goons from the reservation?"

The old man clutched at his shorn braids and wept. "Sam Sweetwater?" Doc mumbled when he recognized Sam's face through the blood and the tears. "They've taken my dignity, boy. First, they stole my honor by forcing me to counterfeit my heritage for them, and then today they come in here and demand I dishonor myself even further with lies in the white man's court."

"Let's get you cleaned up, Doc," Sam said as he helped the weeping old man to his feet. "I'll call your daughter while you wash up in the restroom."

"Hilda's number is on a list taped to my desk," Doc told him as he stumbled into the restroom and flipped on the light.

Sam heard the water running in the bathroom sink as he searched the desk piled high with archeological digests and order forms for trinkets from Chinese manufacturers. Sam rolled his eyes and shook his head, hoping the old man hadn't fallen in with the other shop owners and had resorted to importing their heritage from China too. He found Hilda's number on the faded and dingy list of phone numbers taped to Doc's desk.

"Hello?" a female voice answered.

"Hilda, this is Sam Sweetwater. I'm down at your dad's place, and I think you'd better get down here quick."

"Sam?" she said in an uncertain tone. "Has something happened to Daddy?"

"Someone came in, busted up his shop, and worked him over pretty good. He's in the bathroom cleaning up now, but he's in a pretty bad way and may need to go to the clinic on the reservation to get checked out by a doctor." Sam hesitated. "They cut off his braids, Hilda."

"Oh, my God," she groaned. "I'll be over there right away, Sam." The phone disconnected, and Sam tucked it back into the pocket of his jacket, wondering whether or not he should call the Tribal Police and get them involved in this.

"Hilda's on her way, Doc," Sam said when he walked to the open restroom door. "You have some ice around here? If you do, I'll get some to put on your eye, so you don't end up with a shiner." Sam took his phone out again. "I'm calling the Tribal Police. Nathan and his bunch of goons have gone too far this time."

Doc stayed Sam's hand with his. "Don't bother, boy," the old man said, "about the ice or the phone call."

"Why?" Sam asked in surprise.

"Because Jason Gray Wolf is one of Nathan's Brethren," the old man said as he touched the cut above his swelling eye, "and this will heal soon enough."

"But won't you need a police report for your insurance company?" Sam asked, gazing around at the wrecked cases and shattered pottery in the shop.

Doc snorted. "What insurance? I haven't been able to afford insurance on this place since Nathan and the Brethren started extorting their protection money from me over a year ago."

Sam heard a car pull up outside, and then a woman in jeans and a sheepskin coat rushed inside. "What in the name of heaven happened here, Daddy?" Hilda Silver Eagle gasped as she rushed to her father's side. "Was it that damned Brethren bunch again? Haven't you been paying them their damned fee every month for their protection of this place?"

"It wasn't the tithe this time, Hilda," Doc said as he put his hand to his head. "This time, they wanted more than my money and my products," he wept as he touched the spot on the side of his head where a braid once hung, "and I refused to give it, so they took my dignity." He fell weeping into his daughter's arms.

Hilda glanced up at Sam. "I sure hope you can put an end to this bullshit when you become governor, Sam."

"Oh, I intend to put an end to it now, Hilda. Take your father home, get him bandaged up, and me and the boys will be here in the morning to help you put all of this right again."

"Thank you, Sam," she said as she helped her weeping father to his feet.

Hilda locked up the shattered shop while Sam helped Doc into her car. "I'm so ashamed of what I've done, Samuel," Doc mumbled. "I've soiled my reputation as a man of science and a man of this proud tribe."

"We'll talk about this in the morning, Doc. Go home with Hilda and try to get some rest tonight." Sam shut the car door, waited for Hilda to take charge of her weeping and injured father, and then got into his truck to return home.

"I swear to God I'm gonna beat the shit out of that bastard Nathan as soon as I get my hands on him," Sam swore out loud as he turned the key in the ignition.

When he saw Nathan's truck parked in the lot of Patsy's bar, Sam couldn't resist and turned into the parking lot. Inside the smokey building packed with drinkers from the reservation, the jukebox waled a Hank Williams tune as Sam located Nathan's silver head in the crowd. He sat beside Silvia, dressed in one of her finest outfits, and wore several pieces of Doc's jewelry around her neck. The ear-piercing dings and shrill ringing from the slot machines filled the room.

"Slumming tonight, Mother? Aren't you a bit over-dressed for this dive?" Sam said as he positioned himself behind Nathan.

Silvia stared up at her son. "Nathan is taking me out to eat at the casino when he's done with his business here," she said with an admiring glance at Nathan.

Sam snorted. "You mean you're taking this deadbeat low-life parasite out to dinner, don't you, Mother? This asshole hasn't paid for a meal in years unless you gave him the damned money first."

Sam grabbed the man by the shoulders and pulled him off the barstool. "Oh, he's quite done here, Mother," Sam said before punching Nathan Tyler in the mouth, "but I doubt he'll be in any condition to eat the steak he intended you to buy for him with my damned money." Sam punched Nathan in the face again as Sylvia screamed for him to stop and reached for Nathan as the man crumpled to the floor. He then took out his pocketknife, grabbed Nathan's tightly woven braids, and cut them off at the scalp. "That's for Doc Silver Eagle," Sam said before spitting in Nathan's bruised and bleeding face.

"Samuel Sweetwater," Sylvia gasped as Sam handed her the braids, "what have you done?"

"Why don't you ask your low-life paramour what he and his band of asshat Brethren did to poor Doc Silver Eagle?" Sam demanded of his gaping mother. "They beat him, cut off his braids, and trashed his shop."

"That's a lie," Sylvia shouted when she saw the eyes upon her. "Doc Silver Eagle is a disgrace to this tribe," Sylvia said with a scowl as she wiped the blood from Nathan's face with a paper cocktail napkin. "The Tribal Council is disavowing him from the Tribe for selling his knock-off junk to tourists."

"That's ridiculous," Sam scoffed. "Doc does his best to

reproduce pottery and jewelry like our ancestors produced and not cheap crap imported from China." Sam grabbed one of the silver squash blossom pieces from around Sylvia's neck. "This is as close to an authentic piece as I've ever seen, Mother. How can you accuse Doc of selling cheap junk?" Sam glared at his mother. "Are they throwing out the owners of the other shops as well?"

Nathan rolled over and raised up on his elbow and pointed at Sam. "If you weren't running for Tribal Governor, we'd be tossing your apple ass out of the tribe as well, Sam, for sharing the bed of that white bitch whore of yours, who's trying to steal our sacred Tribal land."

"Is that so?" Sam said before drawing his arm back and delivering a solid punch in Nathan's face again. "Disavow me if you'd like, Chief of nothing. I'm about finished with this Tribe anyhow, and I don't need the monthly casino money as so many others do on the Reservation. I support myself and don't need hand-outs from the Council." He glanced down at his mother as she wiped the blood from Nathan's face. "But I'm getting damned tired of supporting you as well, Nathan."

Samuel Sweetwater," Sylvia screamed and grabbed her son's arm, "What are you doing? Get off your tribe's chief."

Sam glared up at his mother. "This sorry excuse for a human being is no chief of mine, Sylvia,"

"I'm ashamed to call you my son, Samuel," Sylvia snarled at her son as she pushed him away from Nathan.

Sam snorted. "That's fine with me, Sylvia. I'll drop the boxes of clothes you moved into my house with you at your house on the reservation tonight." He stood and kicked Nathan in the hip. "I'm assuming this bastard can give you a ride home from here."

"What are you talking about, Sammy?" Sylvia gasped. "My home is with you."

"Not anymore, Sylvia," Sam said in a loud, clear voice so the quieted crowd could hear. "If you and this scum are tossing me out of the Tribe, then you can move back onto the reservation with him and live in your leaky shack together." He grinned down at his mother. "I hope you'll both be very happy together, but you'll have to make do with your stipends from the casino now because I'm done footing the bills for the two of you from what I make from my business."

❦ 11 ❦

Shannon had no appetite but forced herself to make a ham sandwich and chips late in the morning after working on a plot grid for the new story her publisher had asked about. As she stood at the counter spreading Miracle Whip on the bread, she heard a pickup truck at the gate and went to the door to peek out. She didn't need another visit from the Brethren, but the pickup was Ken's and not the big one belonging to Nathan or the goon from the reservation.

Shannon watched her former husband unlock the gate, open it, and drive inside. She should have changed that lock. Now, what did he want? She'd settled with him in the divorce and given him much more than she thought he deserved. After locking the gate back, Ken got back into his truck and drove toward the cabin.

She wondered how he knew where she'd put it on the property. This location wasn't the spot he'd wanted to put a cabin, but it had the view she liked the best. Shannon smiled as she watched Ken follow the red cinder drive toward the cabin, and she was relieved Sam wasn't there. He hadn't returned since their blow-up a few days earlier, and she'd cried herself to sleep almost every night since.

Home Depot had delivered a truckload of building materials for the greenhouse she'd planned, and she'd picked up the phone to call him and let him know a dozen times but never finished dialing any of those times.

He likely knew she would lose this place to the Zuni and didn't want to waste his time putting up a greenhouse he knew he'd just have to take back down again or watch burn. Tears stung her eyes, and she dashed them away with her hands as Ken pulled up and exited his truck.

"So, you built back here after all," he said, staring at the cabin. "Looks good, I have to admit."

"Thanks," Shannon said uneasily from where she stood, leaning against a redwood porch post. "What are you doing here, Ken?"

He turned his head away from her and pretended to study the array of solar panels on the roof of the storage shed at the end of the drive. "I was wondering if I could pick up the camper," he said, running a hand through his hair and shifting his weight from foot to foot. Shannon recognized the nervous tell. "If you still have it, I mean."

"You and Dale planning a big camping trip for the holidays, or are you gonna haul it down to San Felipe to shack up in while they work on your place down there?" Shannon couldn't resist the dig but knew something was wrong when she saw the hurt expression on her former husband's face as he stepped up onto the porch. "Come on in," she said, "I think the fresh pot of coffee should be ready now."

They walked inside the cabin, and Ken's eyes went to the massive stone fireplace with bookshelves on either side. "Wow," he whistled. "Who'd you get to do all of this? It looks great." He wandered aimlessly through the cabin, taking in everything.

"Sam Sweetwater and his crew did most everything," she admitted, and she wondered for a minute if Ken knew about her and Sam.

Why did she feel so guilty? She and Ken weren't married anymore, and he'd been the one who'd stepped out of their marriage on her. "What's going on, Ken? Why do you want the camper all of a sudden? It didn't come up on your list of wants in the divorce."

He took a deep breath as he petted the buffalo head mounted above the fireplace. "This is a bit gauche, don't you think?" Ken said in an effort to change the subject Shannon recognized well. "Buffalo weren't really in this area much. An elk or antelope head would have been more appropriate. The pottery looks good, though," he said, running a finger over one of the Zuni reproduction pieces she'd picked up from Doc Silver Eagle's shop.

"I found the Buffalo at the antique store I like so much down in the valley," she said, "and he fits with the motif I was going for here."

Ken walked over and peeked into the bedroom. "I see you didn't follow through in there," he said, shaking his head. "Way too girlie for me, but it suits you, Shan."

Shannon poured two cups of coffee and set them on the table. "Are you going to tell me what's going on, Ken? This is the first time you've been up here since—well, since long before that night," Shannon said hesitantly.

"He left me, Shannon," was all Ken said as he picked up his cup of coffee and sipped. "He cleaned out our bank account and just took off. Now the bank is going to take the house, and I'm going to need the camper to live in."

Shannon's mouth fell open in shock. Ken had always been so good with his money. "Why would the bank take the house? I thought we paid it off as a part of the divorce settlement." Shannon grew angry as she thought of something else. "And how the hell did Dale clean out your bank account? Did you open a joint account with him when you always insisted we keep our money separate even after years of marriage?"

Ken's face turned a deep shade of red as he went on to

explain. "I thought he'd be better with money than a woman," Ken said, looking away into the kitchen.

"Better at grabbing what he hadn't earned for himself maybe," Shannon said with a snort, remembering the feel of the weasel-faced man's hands on her throat as he told Ken to take the lottery money from her bag that horrible night. "I have no idea how you could have ended up with a person like that, Ken."

"I put the house up as collateral for the one we're having built in Mexico," he finally said with his head drooping in shame.

"I didn't think you could own property in Mexico if you weren't a citizen," Shannon said. "Did he take everything you won in the divorce?" she asked with her head spinning. "The whole two million?"

"Every penny," Ken said with tears in his eyes. "I'm so sorry, Shannon. I made such a mistake with Dale and ruined all of this for us." He motioned with his hand around the cabin. "But this cowboy off-grid thing was always more your thing than mine, and a house on the beach in Mexico was Dale's."

"So, what was your dream, Ken?" Shannon asked, wondering how she couldn't have known after twenty years of marriage to the man. "If having this quiet place in the mountains to retire to wasn't really your dream, what was it?"

He reached across the table and took her hand. "Having someone to love me and share my life with," he said with tears brimming in his blue eyes. "I made a big mistake, Shannon. Do you think you could ever forgive me and let me come back to share this with you?"

Shannon pulled her hand from Ken's and jumped to her feet. "That ship sailed months ago, Ken." She went to the cabinet with the keys inside and took down the one for the door to the camper.

As she was about to toss it to her former husband, the

front door opened, and Teddy walked inside. "Hey, Shannon," the younger Zuni man said in greeting with an awkward glance at Ken, "Sam wanted me to stop by and see Home Depot had delivered the stuff we ordered for the greenhouse yet."

Shannon found the invoice slip that had arrived with the building materials. "It showed up yesterday and looked like all of it was all there," she said and handed the paper to Teddy. "When do you plan to start?"

Teddy shrugged his shoulders. "I'd start tomorrow," he said, "but Sam said something about waiting until this trial mess was straightened out first." He grinned nervously. "I don't know. I'm just the hired help, but I'd say he has it on the schedule for pretty soon since he had them deliver the materials already." He nodded to the pot. "Think I could get a cup of that coffee to go?"

"Sure," she said and went to the cabinet and took down a ceramic mug with Teddy on the side. Shannon filled the cup and handed it to the native man. "Here ya go, sweety, and thanks for doing such a good job rebuilding the chicken coop."

Teddy took the cup of steaming coffee and smiled. "No problem, Miss Shannon. I just hope I don't have to go chasing those birds around the yard again anytime soon." He nodded at Ken. "She makes the best coffee in Apache County."

"I know," Ken said as he got to his feet and held his hand out for the key to the camper. "I guess I'll take that camper and be on my way."

"You don't want to stay and finish your coffee?" Shannon asked. She couldn't explain why, but Shannon wanted to sit and talk to Ken. He was hurting, and though things had ended between them, she still felt like she wanted to comfort him in some way. "You haven't seen everything yet," she said with a glance around the cabin. Maybe she just wanted to show off what she'd accomplished without his assistance. "I was making myself a sandwich when you drove in. Would you like one before you head back?"

Ken took her hand again. "I'd appreciate that, Shan." He reached for the coffee cup with a trembling hand. "So, tell me what's happening with this thing concerning the Zuni and dead bodies on the property."

"They haven't found any dead bodies yet," Teddy offered, "and Sam says they aren't likely to find any either."

Shannon's eyes went wide. "Why does he say that?" she asked.

Teddy shrugged his shoulders. "This has been a dance site for centuries. A place of rejoicing and happiness for the Zuni," he said, motioning around the property, "and the people wouldn't choose to dance and drink on a sacred burial site." He shrugged again. "Would your people dance and drink in one of your stone-filled burial places?"

Ken snorted. "Some would," he said with a grin at Shannon. She knew he was referring to her and the poor relationship she'd had with her father. She'd never visited his grave and had mentioned more than once that she'd dance on his grave if she ever did, "but for the most part, no, they would not."

"Anyway," Teddy said, shrugging again, "Sam says there are no bodies buried on this property because our people wouldn't make a dance site from a sacred burial site." He emptied his cup. "Well, I'd best go out back and check out those supplies against the invoice." He left the cabin out the back door.

"The Indian seems very familiar with you and this place, Shan," Ken said with irritation in his voice.

"Of course, he's familiar with the place, Ken," Shannon snapped, "he and his friends did all the finish work on this place." She scowled at him. "They did all the things you were supposed to do." Tears ran down her cheeks, and her voice broke with sobs. "All the things we were supposed to do together in our retirement home."

"I said I was sorry, Shannon," Ken said. "I don't know what more I can say. Dale was a mistake, asking for a divorce was a mistake, and letting you go was a mistake. I came up here hoping we could patch things up between us and resume our life together the way it was before all of that."

Shannon shook her head. Did he honestly think he could just waltz back into her life with one silly 'I'm sorry' and expect to be invited in with open arms?

"Just take the camper and go, Ken. I think we're done for good now." She watched him storm back to his truck.

"Dale was right, you know," Ken called out before getting into his truck, "I was entitled to half of that fifteen million and not just a measly two."

Shannon shook her head. "You settled for two in the divorce, Ken. Don't expect any more."

He got into the truck and slammed the door. "We'll see about that," he yelled as he backed the truck up to the camper. Shannon walked to the back door. "You'll be hearing from my attorney, bitch, and this time your scheming bullshit lawyer won't scare me off with embarrassing depositions. Everyone at the school already knows about my relationship with Dale, how you dumped me when you hit it big with the lottery, and how you stole my half of the winnings."

Shannon rolled her eyes as she returned to the cabin and poured herself another cup of coffee. She watched Ken drive away with the camper. She sat down and called Mr. Driscoll to tell him about Ken's visit and his threats to sue for more money.

"Don't worry about that, Mrs. Duncan. The divorce has been settled, and Mr. Duncan signed off on the two million dollar settlement. No judge is going to award him more than he's already agreed to when it comes to light that he allowed his paramour to abscond with it."

As they spoke, Sam walked in, and Shannon's heart leaped into her throat. How did he know she needed him? "Thank you, Mr. Driscoll. That eases my mind some."

"And I think we are as ready as we are going to be as far as the confrontation with the Zuni is concerned."

Shannon clicked on the speaker so Sam could hear the conversation. "Has the professor given you the results yet of the items found on my property?"

Mr. Driscoll cleared his throat. "Well, it appears the items are of an age that makes it appear they are possibly grave goods of a Zuni woman buried in the distant past."

Shannon hung her head. "Is it over then?" she asked with tears choking her voice again. "Should I start packing my things?"

"Let's not get ahead of ourselves, Mrs. Duncan," Mr. Driscoll said in a calming tone. "This old dog still has a trick or two up his sleeve."

Shannon wiped her eyes as she took a paper towel from Sam and blew her nose. "I hope you're right, Mr. Driscoll."

"You just show up at the courthouse looking confident, Mrs. Duncan," the attorney said, "and everything will work out in our favor."

"Thank you, Mr. Driscoll," Shannon said. "I appreciate all you've done for me here."

"It's what you pay me for, Mrs. Duncan. I'll see you Monday morning, and when we're done, you won't have to worry about your property any longer." He disconnected, and Shannon dropped the phone onto the table.

"Sounds like your guy has things well in hand," Sam said as he went to the counter and poured himself a cup of coffee.

"I certainly hope so," Shannon said with a deep sigh. "Does it bother you that the Tribe might lose this case after all?"

Sam settled into one of the chairs at the table. "I've always said there were no remains buried on this property, and I still say that." He reached across the table and took her hand. "I'm sorry for being such an ass, Shannon. My mother had me all hopped up with this governor nonsense, and I shouldn't have taken it out on you."

She smiled across the table. "I think you'd make a great Governor of your people, Sam. Maybe you should think about it."

Sam rolled his big brown eyes. "And do you have a nice Zuni girl picked out for me too?"

"Is that some prerequisite for the position or something?"

"According to Sylvia, it is, and she had a whole list of names for me to check out."

Shannon grinned. "I don't suppose my name is on that list anywhere."

Sam left his chair, put his arms around her, pulled Shannon to her feet, and planted a kiss on her lips. "You're the only one on my list, Shannon Duncan," he whispered as his arms tightened around her, "and if that means I'm not suitable to be the governor of the Zuni, then that's fine with me." He kissed her again. "It's finished between Sylvia and me," he said, "and I'm not running for Tribal Governor. I never was. That was all Sylvia."

Shannon wrapped her arms around his neck and kissed him as she'd never kissed anyone before. "I've missed you, Sam."

"I've missed you too, baby. Was that your camper I saw someone haulin' ass out of here with?" he asked before returning to his chair and his coffee.

"Yes," Shannon said with a sigh, "it was Ken." She spent the next twenty minutes telling Sam Ken's sad story about losing Dale, the house, and all his money.

"Serves the asshole right," Sam said as he refilled their cups.

"I suppose it does," Shannon said with a sigh, "but I hate seeing him in such pain.

❦ I 2 ❦

S am rose early and showered while Shannon slept. She'd tossed and turned most of the night, so he was happy to allow her a little extra time in bed before the need to face this day. He knew Sylvia and Nathan would have a crowd assembled at the courthouse to greet them, and he wished he could spare Shannon that.

He dressed, went to the kitchen, and started coffee. The smell of the brewing coffee woke Shannon, and he waited for her to appear in the living room dressed in a professional blue suit to pour her a cup.

"How are you feeling?" Sam asked as she took a seat at the table and reached for the cup with trembling hands.

"Nervous," Shannon said as she put the cup to her lips.

"Would you like breakfast before we go? I'll even cook."

Shannon shook her head. "I'm too nervous to eat and probably couldn't keep it down," she said. "Coffee will be fine."

An hour before the scheduled court time, they got into Shannon's Jeep and headed for St. Johns, where the courthouse was located. "Don't worry, baby," Sam said as they buckled their seatbelts, "everything is going to be fine today. You'll see."

Shannon flashed him a weak smile. "Thanks, Sam. I appreciate your support, but I'm well aware that it's likely the judge is going to award this land back to the Zuni."

They drove on into St. Johns in silence, and Sam groaned when he saw the crowd of tribesmen standing outside the courthouse. "Just stay close to me as we walk in," he said as he parked the Cherokee.

Shannon kept her head down as they neared the crowd and didn't let her fear get the better of her until someone spit on her and the people yelled racial slurs at her from the group pressing closer and closer. Someone grabbed the sleeve of her jacket and tugged hard. Shannon heard fabric rip as the seam gave way, and she lost her balance on the concrete sidewalk in front of the building. If it hadn't been for Sam's supporting arms, she'd have fallen.

"Just hang in there, Shannon," he whispered as more spit landed in her hair.

"How can you expect us to support you for governor, Sweetwater," someone yelled, "when you're planting your seed in white ground?"

Shannon shrunk from the laughter and felt so sorry for Sam. These were his people, and she'd become an embarrassment for him.

At the door, Sam turned to face the crowd of jeering onlookers. "Let me make this very clear," he called out in a loud voice. "I was never running for Tribal Governor. My mother, Sylvia Sweetwater, and Nathan Tyler, forged my signature and filed the paperwork at the Pueblo in New Mexico and not me."

There was a murmuring in the crowd. "Furthermore," Sam continued, "where I plant my seed is nobody's business but my own." He tightened his grip on Shannon as they turned and entered the courthouse together.

"I think I need to stop in the restroom," Shannon said when she saw the door to the ladies' room.

"Sure," he said and stopped outside the door. "I'll wait for you out here."

Shannon walked into the tiled room that smelled of overly sweet deodorizer, reminding her of the bathroom in her father's old Shell station, and stood in front of the mirror to inspect the damage done by the crowd outside. She first wet a paper towel from the dispenser and swiped it through her hair to remove the spittle deposited there. Then she inspected her torn jacket and took it off. She hoped she could repair it with her sewing machine at home.

The toilet flushed in the stall behind her, and Shannon glanced up to see Sylvia Sweetwater walk out wearing a traditional Zuni three-tiered skirt that went almost to the floor, a simple blouse caught up at the waist with a leather belt ringed with ornate silver conchos, and a shawl woven on a handloom covered in Native designs. Silver jewelry hung at her neck heavy with turquoise and red coral, silver bracelets jingled at her wrists, and her fingers sported their usual array of rings matching the necklaces.

Shannon shook her head as she touched up her makeup after cleaning her face with another dampened paper towel. The old girl was playing the Zuni Tribal woman bit for all it was worth today. Sylvia recognized her, grinned, and left the restroom without washing her hands. Shannon reapplied her lipstick, happy to have avoided a confrontation with the woman. She draped her jacket over her arm and left the room to find that Sam had not been as lucky as her. He stood toe to toe with his mother in the broad hall.

"I've nothing to say to you, Sylvia," he shouted at the woman. "We're done."

"I suppose you'll be moving that white whore into my house with you after the Tribe takes our land back from her," Sylvia shouted, attracting the attention of everyone in the hall.

"Stop making a scene, Sylvia," Sam said, glancing at Shannon with a look that said stay back. "You look and sound like an old fool, ranting in front of everyone like this."

"You're the only fool here, Samuel Sweetwater," Sylvia continued to storm at her son, "and if you continue to carry on with that white tramp, you'll lose your standing in the Tribe completely, especially after what you did to you your Chief the other night at Patsy's." She turned with her head held high and marched off toward the courtroom with her silver jingling, her boot heels clicking on the tiled floor, and her skirt swaying as she walked.

Sam offered Shannon his arm, and she took it as they made their way through the crowd to find a seat in the courtroom filled to overflowing with Zuni Tribe members. Mr. Driscoll sat at a table and motioned them forward to sit with him. In her tribal finery and Nathan with his gray hair cut short and combed back, Sylvia sat at a table beside the attorney hired by the Tribe.

The judge, a tall, thin, negro man with gray hair, walked in, and the bailiff called the court to order to hear the case of the Zuni Tribe vs. Shannon Duncan for the rights to the land they claimed she illegally possessed.

Mr. Driscoll brought forth Shannon's deed as well as the records of the deeds of the former owners of the property to show legal possession by her and white owners in the past going back almost a hundred years.

"Your honor," Mr. Driscoll said, "this piece of property has been in the hands of white owners for nearly a century. If the Tribe suspected there were burials there, why has it never been brought into contention before now?" He lifted the deed in his hand. "This is a legally recorded deed in this very courthouse, and Mrs. Duncan is the legal owner of the property in question."

The Tribe's lawyer stood. He was a younger man with long hair braided on both sides of his head. He wore jeans, a brown corduroy jacket, and a silver bolo over a shirt made from a native printed fabric. Like Sylvia, he was playing the poor Indian card for all it was worth today. Shannon wondered if her suit made her look whiter to the judge and smiled to herself.

"We're not contesting the fact that Shannon Duncan legally purchased the property in question," the young man said confidently. "What we are questioning is whether she has the right to own it at all, considering it is held by the Zuni people to be a sacred site and has been seen as such for centuries with ceremonial dancing taking place there to this day."

"And Mrs. Duncan has graciously offered to allow the ceremonies to continue there," Mr. Driscoll retorted.

Sylvia whispered into her attorney's ear, and the young man stood again. "It's also likely the property is an ancient burial site, Your Honor, and as such should be returned to the Zuni so proper respect can be observed. Having that woman living atop our ancestors is a grievous disrespect of our people and should be put right immediately."

The courtroom crowd voiced their agreement with the attorney, and the judge had to pound his gavel to quiet them. The question of graves on Shannon's property got his attention, however. "Do you have proof of gravesites?" he asked the Tribe's attorney. "Have remains been uncovered?"

"No bones, Your Honor, the Tribal attorney said, "but what archeologists from ASU consider grave goods were found after the last hard rain on Mrs. Duncan's property, leading us to assume there are burials there, as yet uncovered."

"Your Honor," Mr. Driscoll shouted over the crowd, "the items recovered on Mrs. Duncan's property may have come from a burial, but there is no evidence to say that grave was ever on her property at all. It could very well have washed down onto her property from a burial on the Reservation just to the north of her acreage."

The judge had to pound his gavel again to resume order in his court. "You people will be silent in my court, or I will clear this room and hear the remainder of this testimony in my chambers."

The room quieted, and the judge continued. "Has this property been searched for burials?" he asked.

Mr. Driscoll stood. "It has, Your Honor. A team of archeological students from Arizona State University along with their professor searched the site with ground-penetrating radar and found no evidence of burials on the property."

The Tribe's young attorney snorted. "A team paid for by Mrs. Duncan herself with a large donation to the Archeological Department, no doubt. Anything they came up with would be highly suspect, in my opinion."

A distinguished-looking white man with a beard stood. "I resent that, young man," he shouted. "My team and I did a thorough scientific search of that property, and I resent your malicious slander. Mrs. Duncan did not donate to the university and only paid the fees required to make the search the same as you and your Tribe were asked to pay when you enquired but refused."

"Is that true?" the judge asked the young Tribal lawyer whose face changed from one of confidence to one of irritation. "Did your tribe ask the University to conduct a search of this property but then refuse to pay for it, leaving it for Mrs. Duncan to assume the payment?"

"I wasn't aware the Tribe had made such a request of the university," he said with a quick glance at Sylvia, who shrugged her age-sloped shoulders with a sour look on her wrinkled face. "It was her responsibility to defend her assertions, not the tribe's."

"Do you think we should recess so you can confer with your clients to see whether or not there are other things they didn't tell you about?" the judge said with a smirk.

"No, Your Honor," the attorney said with his cheeks

turning red. "At this time, I'd like to call Professor Standish Curry to the stand."

The distinguished gentleman in the gallery stood and made his way to the stand beside the judge, took the oath to tell the truth, and then sat.

"Would you state your name for the record," the attorney in jeans with braided hair asked, "and tell us what it is you have to do with this case, sir?"

"My name is Standish Curry, and I'm a professor of archeology at the University of Arizona in Tempe. Mrs. Shannon Duncan hired us to perform a scientific investigation of her property after some items were discovered there following recent heavy rains."

"I see," the young man said as he walked back to his table and picked up a plastic bag to carry back to the witness. "And are these the items in question, Professor?" He took a small clay pot from the bag, a silver squash blossom necklace, and several silver bangle bracelets, handing them to the professor to inspect.

"They are," the Professor said after examining each one.

The attorney smiled and offered them to the judge to put into evidence. "I assume you did extensive testing of the items at your lab at the university."

"We did," the professor said.

"And what was your conclusion about these items found on Mrs. Duncan's property, Professor Curry?"

"That they were likely the grave goods of a well-respected Zuni woman, possibly buried up to fifteen hundred to two thousand years ago."

The crowd in the gallery got loud, and the judge had to pound his gavel again. "Do I need to clear this courtroom?" he bellowed, glowering at the crowd of onlookers.

Nathan Tyler stood and motioned to the crowd. He'd dressed much like the attorney in jeans, a denim jacket, and a native print shirt. "Please sit, brothers and sisters," he said in a pleading tone, "and remain silent in honor of this reverend grandmother whose grave goods we gaze upon now." The crowd quieted, and Nathan turned to the judge and gave him a silent nod before resuming his seat beside Sylvia.

"Thank you, sir," the judge said, "but this is my court-room, and it's my responsibility to maintain order here. any more outbursts from anybody," he said, directing his gaze at Nathan, "will result in the clearing of this room for the remainder of the proceedings." He moved his gaze to the tribe's attorney. "Carry on, Mr. Dancing Elk."

"Thank you, Your Honor," he said reverently before returning to the Professor. "And what made you think the goods here were from a burial, Professor?"

"The estimated age for one thing," he said, "and the items themselves. They are all things found with female bodies in the graves of Zuni women from that time period."

"And the body?" the attorney pressed. "Where did you think the body of this esteemed woman might be?"

The Professor glanced past the attorney to the table where Shannon sat. "We did not find a body," he said, "though we did an extensive search of Mrs. Duncan's property with ground-penetrating radar. If there was a grave, I'd assume it was on the reservation just north of her property, and the goods washed down from there in the rain."

"You didn't search north of Mrs. Duncan's property?" he asked in an incredulous tone. "Wouldn't that have been the scientific thing to do in this case?"

"We were being paid to search Mrs. Duncan's property, young man, and had no authorization to trespass on the reservation with our equipment."

The attorney smiled as he walked about in front of the witness box. "You mean the Zuni hadn't paid you to give them a favorable report in this matter as Mrs. Duncan had. Don't you, Professor?"

"I take offense at what you're implying, young man," the

professor shot back. "Mrs. Duncan paid the university's deposit on our equipment and the team's lodgings as is required by the university in matters such as this." He glared at the Tribe's attorney. "My reports reflect exactly what we did and didn't find on her property, and there was no evidence of burials recent or ancient on any section. We didn't trespass upon the reservation as there are numerous signs on the fence stating it is a federal offense to do so."

"I'm finished with this witness, Your Honor." the attorney said in a loud voice to be heard over the laughing crowd in the gallery as he strode back to his table where Sylvia and Nathan sat.

The judge had to pound his gavel to quiet the laughter. "I think this would be a good time to break for lunch," the judge said. "Mr. Driscoll can cross-examine this witness after lunch."

"That's fine with me, Your Honor," Mr. Driscoll said as he cleared the table and slid his papers and note pad into a leather satchel before he zipped it. He turned to Shannon and Sam. "Let's have our lunch at that little cafe with the prime rib sandwiches."

Shannon nodded. "Sounds good to me," she said, "but I could really do with a Coke. My mouth is as dry as the desert."

"How do you think it's going?" Sam asked Driscoll as they walked to the attorney's car.

The older man grinned. "It's going just as I'd expected."

❧ 13 ❧

The cafe was packed with the lunchtime crowd from the courthouse, and they had a hard time finding a seat in the small building though the owners had added tables in anticipation of the influx of onlookers regarding this hearing.

Shannon could feel the eyes upon her when they walked in and hoped there wouldn't be a repeat of her arrival at the courthouse that morning. She and Ken had frequented the small establishment for years on their trips north to visit the property, and she'd been a regular customer since relocating, so it was no surprise when the owner motioned her, Sam, and Mr. Driscoll over to a private table near the kitchen generally reserved for staff on their breaks.

It sat behind a low wall separating the main room from the kitchen, and Shannon hoped it would shield them somewhat from the other customers.

"I had the table ready in case you came in," Molly Peterson said as she seated them and gave them menus. She smiled at Mr. Driscoll. "I put the Prime Rib Sandwich on the board as our special today because I knew Driscoll would be in, and it's his favorite."

Mr. Driscoll patted the woman's hand. "You're a doll, Molly, and don't let anybody tell you differently, especially that reprobate husband of yours you have chained to that stove in the kitchen."

The redheaded Molly smiled, and her cheeks flamed red with the compliment. "What can I get for the two of you?" she asked Shannon and Sam in her stilted Irish accent as she studied the people shoving into the tiny space out front. "I'd like to put your orders in before I go out to try and handle this crowd before it gets out of hand."

"We'll both have the prime rib sandwich with fries and a Coke, Molly," Sam said, "and Mr. Driscoll is right. Pete is a damned reprobate," he said with a wink and a grin at the redhead.

"I heard that Sweetwater," a male voice called from the kitchen, and they all laughed.

Their lunch was pleasant until somebody, while paying their check, noticed them behind the counter and began shouting insults. Sam stood and went toe to toe with the jeering man. "There's no need for this nonsense in public, Joe. The judge will decide one way or the other whether Shannon has the right to stay on her land or not."

"That's just it, Sweetwater," the Native man spat while staring at Shannon, "your white whore's got no right to be there in the first place disrespecting our ancestors with her white man's whore parlor where she takes red men like you into her bed."

Shannon had heard enough. She stood, tossed her napkin into her plate, and faced the man at the cash register. "You might want to check your dictionary, sir," she said, glowering at the man, "because if I recall correctly, a whore is a woman who gets paid for her services." Shannon tossed a twenty onto the counter along with their check for lunch, "and I seem to be the one doing all the paying around here, so I think you have it ass-backward in my way of thinking." She slipped her purse over her shoulder and walked through the silent onlookers with her head held high.

There was no repeat of the morning's harassment as they made their way into the courthouse through the rear entrance and walked through the back corridors to get to the courtroom. "I hate slinking around like I should be ashamed of something I've done," Shannon said as they made their way into the courtroom and took their places behind Mr. Driscoll's table.

Sam squeezed her hand. "You've got nothing to be ashamed of, sweetheart," he said, "and everyone is going to know that by the time this day is done."

The gallery filled, the bailiff announced the judge, and Professor Curry resumed his seat in the witness box.

"I'll remind you that you're still under oath, Professor," the judge told him.

"Yes, Your Honor," the Professor said as Mr. Driscoll approached.

"So, what did you find on my client's property, Professor Curry? You say the items found on there were likely grave goods?"

The professor cleared his throat. "We did extensive testing on the items in our lab at the university," he said, glancing at Shannon, "and in my opinion, the items were likely placed in the grave of a prominent woman of the tribe sometime in the sixteenth century."

Driscoll held up the plastic bag containing a clay pot about the size of a modern face cream jar and several pieces of silver jewelry. "But there were no human remains along with these items?" he asked. "Wasn't that strange?"

The professor shook his gray head. "The body would likely have been wrapped in a blanket for burial as was common practice at the time," he said, "and her personal items placed lovingly around her. I'd reckon her body is somewhere north of Mrs. Duncan's property on the reservation. and would recommend the Tribe have an archeological team begin a search before she is further disturbed by the elements."

"Could you explain to us what sort of tests you did on these items to determine their age and authenticity, professor?" Driscoll asked as he returned the plastic bag to the judge's desk.

"Most of the physical testing was done on the clay of the pot. We used Carbon dating of the glaze on the pot to determine its age along with physical comparisons with existing items from certain time periods." He turned to the judge. "We did the same comparisons with the jewelry as there is no way to carbon date the metal or stones in the pieces. The maker's designs are consistent with pieces in our collection recovered from graves dated to the sixteenth century, however."

"I see, Mr. Driscoll said, "and a reputable scientist discovered and dated those items?"

Professor Curry smiled. "Indeed, sir. Professor Silver Eagle from this same area, who was my predecessor in the Archeological Department at the university. I had hoped to see him while I was here to get his opinion on the find at Mrs. Duncan's, but I'm told he suffered a mishap at his place of business and has been indisposed."

"Thank you, Professor," Mr. Driscoll said. "I'm finished with this witness."

The young Zuni attorney stood. "At this time, we rest our case, your honor. It's obvious the property in question is sacred to the Zuni as a hallowed dance site and a burial ground of our people in the distant past. We ask that you return it to our care and move this woman off it."

The gallery erupted in applause and war whoops. The judge banged his gavel to quiet the crowd with anger and irritation etched on his face. "We will hear this case out, young man," he told the attorney. "You were given the opportunity to present your case. It's only fair Mr. Driscoll has the opportunity to present his." He then gazed out at the gallery, pointing his gavel. "One more loud outburst from this crowd, and I'll clear this courtroom of all you for disturbing my proceedings." He pointed the gavel at Mr. Driscoll. "You may proceed with your case, Mr. Driscoll."

Thank you, Your Honor," he said respectfully. "At this time, I'd like to call Professor Jason Silver Eagle to the stand."

Sam watched from where he sat as Nathan Tyler bent to whisper in the Tribal attorney's ear, and the young man jumped to his feet. "I object, Your Honor. This man is not on my witness list, and I've had no time to prepare for what testimony he might have to offer this court."

"Is there some good reason this witness' name was not supplied to the Tribe, Mr. Driscoll?" the judge asked with a frown.

"As you just heard, Your Honor, Doctor Silver Eagle recently suffered an injury, and we didn't think he was going to be available to testify."

"But he's recovered now?" the judge asked.

"He is, Your Honor," Driscoll said with a glance at the other table where Nathan Tyler continued to whisper into the attorney's ear.

"I persist in my objection to the addition of this witness, Your Honor," the young attorney grumbled. "He can't possibly have anything to offer more than his verification of Professor Curry's findings, and that would simply be a waste of the court's time."

The judge raised a gray brow. "If that is truly the case, young man, then I should think you'd be eager to have that testimony to back up your claim the property in question holds tribal burials." His eyes returned to Mr. Driscoll. "You may call your witness."

Doc walked into the courtroom with his daughter at his

side. He wore a bandage on his forehead, and his eye was blackened all the way down his left cheek. Sam knew it must be painful and felt for the old man. He'd suffered broken ribs in the attack at his store and had remained at his daughter's home where Hilda thought he'd be safe from Nathan and the Brethren.

"Please state your name for the record, sir," Mr. Driscoll asked.

"Doctor Jason Silver Eagle," Doc said as his age-spotted, trembling hand went to the spot on his head where a braid once hung.

"And what is your profession, Doctor Silver Eagle?" Driscoll asked.

"I own a tourist shop on the highway across from the reservation," he said with a glance at Nathan and Sylvia. "A tourist shop, I'm told, is such a disgrace to my tribe I've been swept from the Tribal rolls as a member."

"I'm sorry to hear that, Doctor Silver Eagle."

The Tribal attorney jetted to his feet. "I call this witness's testimony into question, Your Honor. He has to be holding a grudge against the Zuni for disavowing him, and as such, brings any testimony he may have to offer into question. I strongly object to this witness."

The judge addressed Doc Silver Eagle. "Can your testimony be relied upon, Sir," he asked, "or should I dismiss you now?"

"I've always prided myself on my honesty, Sir, and I have no reason to change that now," he said with a glance at Nathan. "No matter my personal circumstances with regard to the Zuni."

The Tribal attorney snorted. "I highly suspect that, Your Honor. Why would we believe this bitter, disavowed man?"

"Why indeed?" the judge sighed. "Doctor, you do realize you are under oath to tell the truth."

"I do, Your Honor, and my testimony is no less trustworthy than that of my esteemed colleague Dr. Curry."

The judge nodded. "Thank you, Doctor Silver Eagle," he said and then nodded to Mr. Driscoll. "Carry on, Mr. Driscoll, and present your questions to this witness."

Mr. Driscoll smiled. "Thank you, Your Honor." Driscoll addressed his witness. He picked up the plastic bag of grave goods and carried them to Doc. "Will you study these for us, Doctor, and tell the court if you agree or disagree with Professor Curry that they are the grave goods of a Zuni woman buried in the sixteenth century?"

Doc Silver Eagle removed each item from the bag, studied them, rotated them, and carefully looked at each piece. After a few minutes of study, Doc set the items on the rail around the witness box. "I've seen enough," he said.

"And do you concur with Professor Curry?" Driscoll asked as folks in the gallery murmured amongst themselves about what the popular reservation citizen would answer.

Doc grinned. "I'm honored that such an esteemed archeologist would see these items as ancient," he said. "But they are not."

"And what exactly do you mean by that, Doctor? Are they not ancient?" Mr. Driscoll asked.

"It's certainly what I intended them to look like when I made them," Doc said with a chuckle as the gallery erupted.

"Excuse me?" Professor Curry said as he jumped to his feet. "Those items are ancient, and I'd stake my reputation on it."

"What exactly are you saying, Doctor Silver Eagle?" Mr. Driscoll asked as the judge pounded his gavel to try and quiet the gallery again. "What do you mean that you made them?" he asked as he picked up the little pot.

"My store is or was," he said, glaring at Nathan Tyler, "until Tyler and his Brethren bastards broke in one night and trashed it, a place where tourists could purchase items of authentic manufacture and design." He raised the little pot. "My pottery is evidently so authentic it could fool a renowned professor such as my good friend Doctor Curry, and I'm truly sorry for making you look the fool in this court, sir."

"Why would the reservation's Brethren, as I understand they call themselves, come into your place of business, destroy it, and deliver a beating to you, Doctor?" Mr. Driscoll asked in a sympathetic tone.

"I refuse to listen to these lies," Nathan yelled, jumping to his feet. He motioned to some men in the gallery, and they stood as well. "This bitter old man holds no standing in our community, and his lies shouldn't be given any credence.

The judge pounded his gavel. "Gentlemen," the judge said in a commanding voice, "please resume your seats until this witness finishes his testimony, or I'll have you charged with contempt."

"I have nothing but contempt for this white man's court," Nathan snarled and continued toward the door.

"Stop that man," the judge called to his bailiff, who pulled his firearm and charged toward Nathan only to be cut off by the Brethren who stepped in front of him, scowling and flexing their muscles.

"It's all right, Howard," the judge called out, "I buzzed for the State Police Officers in the courthouse, and they'll be crashing this little war party any minute now."

A few minutes later, three officers in brown uniforms burst through the doors with their weapons drawn. "What seems to be the trouble in here, Judge?" one of the officers asked as he stopped Nathan at the door.

"Will you take these troublemakers into custody, Jeff, and put them into the cells down below until this hearing is concluded at least."

"Yes, sir," he said as he cuffed Nathan and the other officers, along with the bailiff, took the Brethren members into custody.

"Let's get back to the business at hand," the judge said with a sigh when the room had quieted again. "Shall we?"

"Would you elaborate on your statement of before this interruption, Doctor?" Mr. Driscoll asked. "Were you telling the court that the items found on Mrs. Duncan's property were not in actuality ancient Zuni artifacts, but items manufactured by yourself for sale in your store?"

The old man straightened in his seat. "That's exactly what I'm trying to tell you." He coughed to clear his throat as the judge hammered his gavel to quiet the astounded gallery again. When the room was still once more, he continued. "A few weeks ago, Nathan Tyler and his Brethren goon squad from the reservation showed up at my shop and demanded I give them an assortment of items to use against Mrs. Duncan."

"And Mr. Tyler thought these fraudulent antiquities would fool modern scientists?" Driscoll asked.

Doc grinned with a glance into the gallery at Professor Curry, who sat with his mouth open in shock. "I studied the antiquities of my people for decades," he said, "and when I opened my shop, I promised my dear wife Ella to give the people coming to visit our land only the very best." His glance shifted to Sylvia. "I do not sell knock off imitations of what my ancestors created. You won't find any of that cheap crap from Hong Kong on my shelves." He gave the old woman a smug nod. "I mark all my work in the same way," he said, "and I only offer the very best to my customers. When they take something home from my shop, they are getting something that could have been created by one of my ancestors and put into the ground centuries ago."

Mr. Driscoll removed the little pot from the banister in front of him and handed it to Doc. "Can you show us this mark, Doctor?"

Doc carefully took the pot and turned up to examine the bottom. He then pointed to a spot. "All my work has this eagle glyph," he said. "I put it on the bottom of all my pots and stamp it into all my jewelry pieces. You'll find it stamped into the inside of the center squash blossom on that piece," he said with a nod at the heavy Zuni necklace in Driscoll's hand. "If you examine the necklace around Miss Sweetwater's neck over there," he said, nodding at Sylvia, "you'll find one there as well."

Sam grinned when he noticed women in the crowd removing pieces of their jewelry to inspect them for the same maker's mark. Doc Silver Eagle had sold a good many pieces on the reservation, it seemed.

The judge pounded his gavel to quiet the room again and cleared his throat. "Do you have any further evidence to present, young man?" he asked Sylvia's wide-eyed attorney.

"That old fraud is lying, Judge," Sylvia yelled, pointing a ringed finger at Doc. "He's pissed at the tribe for booting him out and denying him his cut of the casino profits. Those grave goods on that white whore's land prove it is sacred to our Tribe and should be returned to us." She pounded a bony fist on the table."

"Please take your seat, madam," the judge said, "and stop acting a fool in my court."

Sam grinned as his mother dropped back into her chair. "I should have known we'd receive no justice in this white man's court," she hissed, glowering at the judge.

"I'm ready to deliver my verdict," the judge said with a sigh as the bailiff directed the people at the tables to stand for the delivery of the judge's verdict. "I find in favor of Shannon Duncan in this matter, and her property is to remain in her possession." He said with a scowl at Sylvia. "The tribe is also directed to reimburse her for all costs associated with this case as well as remit court costs to the government." He pounded his gavel. "We are adjourned," he said before stepping down from the bench and leaving the room, followed by his bailiff.

Sam wrapped his arms around Shannon. "I told you things would work out, baby," he whispered before kissing her hard on the lips.

"I'm just glad it's over," Shannon said, slumping into his strong arms.

Sylvia took the opportunity at that time to voice her opinion. "This isn't over, whore," she yelled at Shannon. "We'll appeal this verdict and tie you up in court until all your money is gone."

Some in the crowd cheered the old woman, but Sam had heard enough. "You lost, Sylvia," he yelled at his mother, "just give it a rest and go back to your hovel on the reservation where you belong, or it will be your fault the people lose their monthly dividend checks from the casino."

The room quieted as they considered his words. "Where do you think the money is going to come from to reimburse Shannon and the court for Sylvia's little court case here?" he called out. "It's coming out of your pockets by way of your monthly checks." Sam shook his head. "I don't suppose any of you ever considered that, did you?"

"You're a disgrace, Samuel Sweetwater," Sylvia yelled with tears running down her wrinkled face. "No decent Zuni would vote for you to be our governor when you have your manhood stuck between the legs of this white whore and run to her aid whenever she calls, turning your back on your own people for her." Sylvia spat on the floor. "You're not your father's son, Samuel, and you're no longer a son of mine."

Sam rolled his eyes. "Being Governor was never a dream of mine, Sylvia, and if you want it that so badly, why don't you run yourself." He glanced at Shannon with a grin. "I doubt you have the funds to finance a campaign, though, since Nathan is such high upkeep and all."

Tears filled the old woman's eyes, and Sam almost felt

sorry for her had he not seen her use this ploy before so many times. "You're an evil young man, Samuel, to treat the woman who bore you and raised you alone like this."

"Sylvia, I've heard this all before, so just give it a rest," Sam scolded and took Shannon's hand. "Let's get out of here, Shan, since I'm no longer a part of this Tribe," he said, glaring at his mother, "or a part of her family."

❧ 14 ❧

Shannon was overjoyed and relieved to have the court case behind her and hoped her troubles with the Zuni and the Brethren were over as well. She wasn't so certain of that when she noticed the large blue pickup following them out of town.

"It looks like Nathan's Brethren are on our tail," Shannon told him, and Sam glanced up into the rearview mirror of Shannon's Jeep Cherokee.

"Shit," he growled and pulled the Jeep over onto the side of the road. "I've about had my fill of these assholes," Sam said as he got out of the Jeep and slammed the door. Shannon released her seatbelt to turn in her seat to watch what was going on behind the Jeep. The big Indian who drove the monster truck jumped out and charged Sam as two others shambled out after him.

"What you gonna do now, big political man of the tribe?" the big Zuni said, flexing his fingers and then balling them into ham-like fists as he moved through the knee-high weeds along the paved road. "We're gonna beat the shit out of you, and then," he said, grinning at Shannon, "we're gonna all get a taste of your white whore."

The others laughed as Sam turned to Shannon. "Get back in the car, Shan, and lock the damned doors."

"It's all right, Sam," Shannon said, lifting the fully loaded 357 she'd taken from the glove compartment, "I've got this." She cocked the shiny gun and pulled the trigger. The bullet missed the big man and his friends, but it shattered the windshield of the idling pickup. "I suggest you fellas go on home before my aim gets better and all y'all end up in the clinic or worse," she grinned at the looks of shock and disbelief on their faces, "the county morgue."

The two smaller men turned and ran back to the truck, where they scurried over the tailgate and into the bed of the truck. The big Indian stood glaring at Sam and Shannon. She could see the desire in his eyes to use his clenched fists on both of them, but he turned his head to see the shattered glass of his windshield. "This is war, bitch, and I'm gonna take you out if it's the last thing I do," he thundered before jogging back to the truck and roaring off.

Sam took Shannon's trembling arm with the gun held tight in her hand and gently took it from her. "I'm so sorry, Shannon," Sam said and kissed her head. "Let's go home."

Shannon slumped into his arms and let him lead her back to the Cherokee. "Home sounds good," she said as she slid down into the heated leather seat and fastened the seatbelt. "I just want to soak in a hot shower and then have some hot chocolate spiked with Jack Daniels in front of a fire."

Sam chuckled. "That sounds good to me too."

Before they reached the turnoff to Shannon's property, Sam's phone rang. He picked it up and smiled. "It's just Teddy," he said and swiped the screen to answer. "Hey, man, you call to congratulate Shannon on her big win?" He went silent as he listened to Teddy. "Damnit," he hissed and threw the phone into the console between the seats.

"What is it?" Shannon asked, knowing the news couldn't be good. "What's happened?"

He slammed on the brakes and whipped the car around on the blacktop. "My damned house is on fire," he said as he pressed down on the gas pedal and sped toward his property on the outskirts of St. Johns near Lyman Lake.

Shannon had never seen Sam's house because of the tension between her and his mother. "Has Sylvia moved out?" she asked uneasily.

"Yeah, I packed up the last of her stuff and dumped it off at her reservation hovel last week." He shook his head. "I wouldn't put this past the old bitch and her lover," he spat. "It's just the sort of thing they'd do to get even with me for throwing her scrawny red ass back on the reservation where she came from."

Shannon's breath caught in her throat. Would they go so far as burning down her house as well? Both Nathan and Sylvia had to be upset over losing the court case, and Sylvia hated her for her relationship with Sam. They drove up Sam's street and saw black smoke billowing up into the blue sky. and fire trucks spraying water on Sam's doublewide. "I'm so sorry, Sam," Shannon said with a sigh. "This is all my fault."

"Don't be silly," he said as he exited the Cherokee and headed for the man who seemed to be in charge. Shannon got out of the car and joined him. "This is Sylvia all the way," he said and took her hand. They walked up to the Fire chief. "I'm Samuel Sweetwater, and this is my house."

"I'm sorry, Mr. Sweetwater, but I fear she's a total loss. I hope you're insured."

Sam nodded. "I have coverage through State Farm."

The chief lifted his brow. "Were you moving out, Mr. Sweetwater?"

Sam shook his head. "No, why?"

The man shifted from foot to foot. "Well, when my guys went in to spray down the inside, they didn't find any appliances in the kitchen or other furniture like televisions in the house." He scratched his chin. "It looks like the central air unit has been removed from the concrete pad, and the water heater and furnace are missing as well." He coughed. "They didn't find any furniture to make the place livable at all."

"Jeez," Sam hissed, "it sounds like Sylvia is totally remodeling her damned shack with my appliances and furniture."

"Sylvia?" the chief asked. "Do you know who might be responsible for this, Mr. Sweetwater?"

"My mother," Sam muttered, looking away.

"Well, this is a classic case of arson, Mr. Sweetwater, in which case your insurance won't pay out, and the perpetrators will be looking at several years in prison."

A few minutes later, a police vehicle drove up, and the officer put his head together with the fire chief, and they kept throwing suspicious glances at Sam. Shannon squeezed his hand and whispered, "I think they are gonna try and pin this fire on you, babe."

The officer approached them. "I'm afraid I'm going to need to detain you, Mr. Sweetwater."

Sam's eyes went wide. "Detain me?" he gasped. "What the hell for?"

"Suspicion of arson," he said, reaching for Sam's arm as he unhooked handcuffs from his belt.

"Sam was with me all day yesterday," Shannon said, stepping forward to confront the officer, "and he was with me at the courthouse in St. Johns all morning with half the local Zuni tribe and a judge in attendance. There's no way he could have burned down his house."

"I still need to take him into custody to question him," the officer said with a glance at the burning house. "I was told he might know who is responsible for this."

"I'm more than happy to help you with this investigation," Sam said, "but you don't need to handcuff me."

"It's simply procedure, sir," the officer said, "but if you promise to cooperate, I suppose we can go in without the cuffs."

"No problem," Sam said and turned toward the vehicle.

"I'm going to run back to the house," Shannon said to Sam, "and make sure my appliances are all still there."

"Be careful, Shannon," Sam said before releasing her hand. "Nathan and Sylvia's thugs with the Brethren might be out for blood now with the loss of that damned lawsuit."

The officer gave Shannon an appraising glance. "You the one in court with the Zuni?" he asked. "If you are, he's right, ma'am. I hear they're out for blood because you beat their behinds." He grinned. "Good for you, but you should be very careful."

Shannon rolled her eyes. Would it never end? "I'll be fine," she said with a grin and patted the 357 in the holster on her hip. "My little friend here has dealt with those ass hats before and come out on top."

The officer frowned, noticing the gun for the first time. "You have that thing registered, ma'am?"

Shannon grinned. "All nice and legal," she said and then kissed Sam's cheek. "I'll be careful, babe, and I'll see you when this fine young man is finished with you." She turned to the officer. "You'll drive him home when you're finished asking your questions?"

He glanced from Shannon's smiling face down to the big pistol on her hip. "Yes, ma'am, as soon as my questions are all answered."

Shannon nodded and got into the Cherokee. She watched the police vehicle drive away with Sam in the back. Shannon put the Cherokee in gear and drove toward her property—the property the law said was actually hers. She kept her eyes peeled for the big pickup and Nathan Tyler's SUV and let out a sigh of relief when she pulled into her drive and found her home intact.

Shannon got out of the car, secured the new steel gate, drove on to the cabin, and hurried inside. Everything appeared undisturbed, and she breathed another sigh of relief.

The hot shower called to her, but Shannon thought she should attend to things around the house first and went outside to feed her chickens and collect eggs.

As she scattered feed to her clucking hens, Shannon heard the racing of an engine. She craned her neck to see the big pickup at her gate, and her heart began to race. Why wouldn't these pricks just give it a rest? They'd lost their court case. What did they hope to gain by harassing her now? Shannon moved to the corner of the cabin and peeked around to see three men climbing the fence and jogging toward the cabin. One was the big driver, and the two others following were the smaller men from their confrontation earlier in the day.

"Come on out, whore," the big man called "and see what real red men can do with you."

Shannon made her way into the cabin and yelled through the open window. "If I saw any real red men out there, I might."

"I hope you have that pea shooter with you bitch," he called back, "because I brought a real gun with me this time." He lifted a semi-automatic pistol and sprayed the front of the cabin.

Shannon dropped to the floor and rolled away as bullets pinged around her in the small cabin. Her doors were locked, but she heard glass shattering in the bedroom's French door. She positioned herself with the gun aimed at the bedroom door.

"How does Sweetwater even get it up in a room like this?" she heard one of them ask with a chuckle. "I think I'll fuck the bitch on the damned floor in the living room."

"Come on out, bitch, and take your medicine," the big man called as he laughed and squeezed his crotch.

Shannon aimed and squeezed the trigger, taking down the big man with the pistol in his hand. One of the others lunged for his dropped machine pistol, and Shannon fired again. She missed, and he raised the pistol, spraying bullets in her direction. She slid behind the safety of her oak kitchen cabinets but felt a searing pain in her hip. Shannon gasped in pain, fired wildly around the edge of the cabinet, and felt someone fall to the floor.

"I'm scootin' out of here, lady," she heard one of the other men say. "I just gotta come back in and grab Mal's keys to the truck." He tossed the pistol out onto the living room floor and walked in with his hands up. "Don't shoot me, lady, and I'll book on out of here once I get his keys."

"Get 'em and get the hell off my property," Shannon said in a trembling voice as blood pooled on the tile floor around her.

The young man took the keys from the big Indian's belt and hurried out of the cabin through the open bedroom doors. Shannon dug the phone from her pocket and punched in Sam's number.

"I'm still a little busy here, babe," Sam said in an irritated voice. "Shannon?" he added when she didn't reply with more than heavy, labored breathing.

"They shot me, Sam," she grunted in a painful, trembling whisper before the darkness took her.

❈ 15 ❈

"What do you mean they shot you, Shannon?" Sam yelled into the phone. "Shannon? Shannon?"

"What's going on, Mr. Sweetwater?" Detective Lawrence asked with his brow furrowed in concern. "Mr. Sweetwater?"

Sam jumped to his feet. "Shannon, Mrs. Duncan, out at her place on Old Hunt Road," he said in an urgent tone, "says she's been shot by some of Nathan Tyler's Brethren idiots. I need to get out there, and you need to send a damned ambulance out there to help her."

The detective yelled into the adjoining room. "Les, get in here and give Mr. Sweetwater a ride to his girlfriend's house since he doesn't seem to own one anymore."

The officer who'd driven Sam to the station in St. Johns came to the door and beckoned Sam to follow him.

"You can sit in the front this time," the officer said when they got to the car. "To hell with their ridiculous regulations out here in the sticks."

Sam opened the passenger side door and got in, securing himself in the seatbelt. "You come to Apache county from somewhere else?"

"Went into the academy in LA," he said, "and worked in LA county for twelve years before my wife's parents got sick, and we moved here to take care of them."

Sam smiled. "This must have been some culture shock."

The officer, at least ten years Sam's junior, rolled his eyes. "That's putting it mildly."

They drove away from the station, and Sam gave him directions to Shannon's cabin. "It's usually pretty peaceful around here, but all this business with Shannon's property has things stirred up like a badger in a beehive."

"It's more than that," the officer said, offering Sam his hand. "I'm Les Peterson, Mr. Sweetwater, and my wife is—or was Emily Black Claw. She was really hoping you were going to run for Governor to put an end to all the tribal bullshit going on these days."

Sam's eyes went wide. "I know Emily. She was in one of my late wife's elementary school classes on the reservation before Karla was killed in an accident on the highway. What has her trouble with the Tribe?"

"Well, for one thing, they booted her off the tribal rolls because she married me, and her parents left the reservation."

"James and Mary Black Claw left the reservation years ago," Sam said in surprise. "That's no reason to scratch Emily from the tribal rolls."

"They said her mother wasn't Zuni, and so by Tribal Law, she didn't qualify to be called Zuni any longer." He shook his head. "I think her mom was half Zuni and half Navajo with some Apache in there somewhere as well or something like that."

Les snorted. "It's all about those monthly checks from the casino. There are those in the tribe who want a bigger share, so they're tossing people off the rolls right and left to raise their cuts."

Sam shook his head. "That sounds like Nathan Tyler's

doing," he said. "I wonder how his bloodline would stand up if it came right down to it."

"What do you mean?" Les asked as he passed a truck with his lights and siren on.

"His grandmother," Sam said, "was married to a white man, and his mother wasn't married at all. I'm not quite certain who his father was or from what tribe if any."

"Maybe someone should get him one of those Ancestry DNA tests," Les said with a grin as they turned onto the dirt road leading toward Shannon's.

When they got to Shannon's locked gate, Sam got out and unlocked it. Les drove up to the cabin. "Damn, it looks like this place went through a firefight," Les said, noting the bullet holes in the walls of the cabin and the shattered windows. Sam ran into the cabin through the open bedroom door, and Les followed.

"Shannon," Sam called out as he stepped over the bodies of the two bloody Brethren. "Shannon," he called again, and his breath caught in his throat when he saw her foot sticking out from behind the kitchen cabinet and the pool of blood on the floor. "Where the hell is that damned ambulance?" he yelled to Les. "She's been shot and losing blood," he said in desperation as he grabbed a dish towel and pressed it to the wound in Shannon's hip.

Les kneeled beside Shannon and felt her neck for a pulse. "Her pulse is weak, but she has one," he said with a sigh and then called on his radio to see where the ambulance was.

"We were at that location," someone replied, "but the gate was locked, and nobody responded when we honked."

"Damnit," Sam growled, "she was on the floor, bleeding out, you assholes."

"The gate is open now," Les replied. "I have a woman here who's been shot in the hip. She's unconscious and lost a lot of blood. I also have two dead men here, so we'll need the coroner as well and a detective." Les turned to Sam. "I guess we'll need to call the reservation police as well since those two in there, I assume, came from there."

Sam nodded. "Two of their worst troublemakers. The reservation police will know who they are to make the necessary notifications."

Les nodded and made the call to the reservation police office. "My boss isn't gonna be happy," he said as they heard sirens coming up the remote dirt road. "He hates dealing with that guy on the reservation and the Feds when the natives are involved." He gazed around the room at the spray of bullet holes in the walls and the blood on the floor. "And this mess has Feds written all over it."

Sam wanted to ride in the ambulance with Shannon, but the attendants wouldn't allow it. They told him to follow or just meet them at the hospital later. They took all the information about Shannon he could give them, and they told him she would certainly need surgery to repair the bullet wound. The ambulance rushed away with sirens wailing, and Sam stood helpless beside the deputy.

Sam stared around the cabin and wondered if he should try to clean up the mess. Les stopped him. "Leave it until the detectives, and the feds get here and take their pictures, Sam."

"She's gonna be so pissed about this mess," he said." We just got it all put together a few months ago, and she was so proud of how nice it turned out."

Les ran a finger over a bullet hole in the drywall. "I think you can patch and repaint the drywall easy enough, but some of those cabinets are beyond help, and the appliances are done for." He shook his blonde head. "This place looks like a damned war zone."

The Reservation cops were the first to arrive. "What the hell happened here, Sweetwater?" Jonas Graywolf demanded when he stormed inside and saw the two bodies on the floor. "Did you shoot my cousins, or was it your white whore, Sweetwater?" he said, staring around the room in search of Shannon.

"Those assholes came in here shooting off an automatic weapon," Les said. "How is it they have weapons like that on the reservation, Graywolf?"

Jonas Graywolf grimaced. "Yeah, you white bastards can have all the guns you want out there," he said, "but we Indians are locked away here on our reservation and left with our bows and arrows or maybe a damned b-b gun to hunt with."

"Don't get carried away, Jonas," Sam said, rolling his eyes. "You know you're allowed hunting rifles and shotguns." He pounded his fist on the countertop. "Just look at what they did to her house, Jonas, and then the bastards shot her."

Jonas snorted as he glanced at the deputy. "The whore's been camped out here on sacred Tribal land for too damned long now and deserved what she got if you ask me." the Tribal officer said with a smirk. "It's just too bad they won't charge her for the murders of my cousins."

"The court just ruled," the deputy said, "that this land belongs to Mrs. Duncan and not the Zuni," Sam said. "Nathan's assholes had no reason to keep bothering her."

Jonas spat on the floor next to the pool of Shannon's blood that hadn't been disturbed by the ambulance crew. "She's a white slut and has no business here on our sacred dance grounds." He glared at Sam. "And you're a race traitor who has no business governing our people if you prefer a white bitch over your own kind."

Sam balled up his fists. He'd heard enough of this bullshit. "Shannon Duncan is one of the finest people I've ever known, Graywolf, and I'm proud to know her. If that makes me unfit to govern this tribe, then I can say I'm glad they've decided to throw me off the rolls too."

Jonas Graywolf snorted. "Tribal members who consort with whites have no place on our rolls if they lower themselves to mix their blood with that of our oppressors and give them children."

The deputy's face grew dark, and he threw a punch at the Tribal officer that sent him into the cabinets and added to the wreckage in Shannon's kitchen. "My wife is as much Zuni as any of the rest of you on that reservation," he snarled, "and you had no right saying she wasn't just because she married me."

Sam grabbed his arm before he could deliver another punch. "The bastard's not worth it, Les," Sam told him. "Just go outside and wait for the investigators to get here."

Jonas struggled to his feet. "I don't need you to fight my battles for me, Sweetwater," he admonished as he rubbed his swelling jaw.

Sam chuckled. "I was going to let the boy beat your ass, Jonas, but he and his wife don't need that bullshit in their lives right now. They just had twins, and I don't think the new daddy is getting much sleep."

"Emily is just another race traitor whore," he spat before Sam sent him into the table and chairs with another punch that left the nose on Jonas's face in an awkward position.

"Make one more comment about either woman, Jonas," Sam warned, "and you'll be breathing out of your asshole from now on."

The tribal police chief got to his feet again with blood streaming from his nose. "You're finished, Sweetwater," he snarled at Sam. "I'll make sure you rot in jail for assaulting a police officer."

Sirens could be heard in the distance as the Federal Agents and the ambulances to take away the dead Brethren approached. "You might want to have one of those EMTs try to put your nose back in the right spot on your pretty face, Jonas," Sam said with a chuckle, "because from where I'm standing, it ain't so pretty anymore."

Jonas took a swing at Sam and missed, falling into the

table once more and upending chairs. Les stuck his head in the door. "What in the name of heaven is going on in here?"

Sam shrugged. "Jonas here just lost his footing for a minute and fell into the table."

"Face first, it would appear," Les said with a grin and a wink at Sam.

❦ 16 ❦

Shannon woke in a state of confusion and pain. She heard voices but didn't know where she was. Then it came back to her in flashes, and she heard the pinging of bullets all around her and the breaking glass of her windows as they shattered around her.

The beeping of a monitor alerted a nurse, and soon the room filled with people talking all at once, asking her about her pain levels and how many fingers they were holding up in front of her face.

"Good grief, will you all please just be quiet. Somebody shot me in the hip, not the damned head. Where is Sam?" she groaned and then fell back onto her pillow to drift back into painless oblivion.

When she woke again, someone was taking blood from her arm. "What time is it?" Shannon asked groggily when she saw only darkness outside the window.

"Well, hello there," the young native woman said with a smile. "It's about three, but I know the nurses have been waiting for you to wake up again. Can you tell me your name and date of birth?"

"Aren't you supposed to ask me that before you poke me

full of holes?" Shannon said as she tried to wipe the crusty film from her eyes.

"I tried," the technician said with a cordial grin, "but you weren't responding. Name and birthdate, please, so I know I've stuck the right person."

"Did someone shoot me?" Shannon asked and then replied with her name and birthdate.

"That's what they said on the news, Mrs. Duncan," she said as she applied tape to a cotton ball on Shannon's arm, "but my husband Les said you acquitted yourself well and took out both the bastards right there in your living room."

Shannon squeezed her eyes shut and remembered pulling the trigger of her 357 as two men approached with their weapons drawn. "They shot up my house," Shannon mumbled more to herself than anyone else as tears of frustration stung her eyes, "And I just got it fixed up the way I wanted it."

"And I can't think of a better reason to blow Malcolm Tagert and Will Gray Wolf away than that." She patted Shannon's arm. "But Les says that fellow asleep on the couch over there is fixing things back up real nice for you out there."

Shannon turned her head to see an unmoving bulk stretched out on the couch across from the bed and the long black hair escaping from the blanket told her it was Sam. "How long has he been here?" she asked.

"Ever since they brought you in from surgery yesterday," the woman said and offered her hand. "I'm Emily Peterson," she said, "and Sam and I have known one another since I went to elementary school on the reservation, and his wife was my teacher."

Emily walked over and gently shook Sam's shoulder. "She's awake, Sam."

Sam sat up and looked around as though he didn't know where he was for a minute, and then he was at her side. "Are you alright, Shannon?"

"Other than a throbbing in my hip that hurts like hell," she said, "I guess I'm OK."

A nurse walked into the room and shooed Sam away from the bed. "I need to get her vitals," she said and manhandled a blood pressure cuff onto Shannon's arm before shoving a thermometer between her lips. "How is your pain level," the nurse asked. "On a scale of one to ten, where would you rate it if one were mild and ten was excruciating?"

Shannon concentrated on the throbbing in her hip. "About a seven, I'd say, but it's very uncomfortable."

"Nothing you shouldn't be able to deal with then, so I'll just leave the two of you to it but keep it down because this is a hospital and sick people are trying to sleep," the nurse said with a scathing glance at Sam before turning and marching out of the room.

Shannon looked at Sam with the throbbing in her hip suddenly on her mind. "What do you think that was all about?"

He rolled his sleepy brown eyes. "Zuni aren't the only ones who have issues with the mixing of the races around here." He took her hand. "I've been so worried about you, Shannon," he said with tears brimming in his eyes. "Please don't do that again."

Shannon flinched with the pain when she tried to adjust herself in the bed and smiled. "I will most definitely try to avoid big, bad, Indians with automatic weapons in the future." She thought for a minute, remembering the pinging of the bullets as they sprayed the cabin. "My house is a wreck now, isn't it?"

"It's seen better days," Sam told her, "but the boys and I are working our asses off to try and put it back to the way you had it." He smiled as he squeezed her hand. "We even have a new member of our crew," he said. "Emily's husband Les has been helping us out, and it doesn't hurt that he's an Apache County deputy sheriff either."

"Do you really think that will keep Nathan and his Brethren away?" Shannon asked.

"The Feds have been all over this since it happened, and I think Jonas Graywolf will try and keep those Brethren knuckleheads in line just to get them out of his hair." He squeezed her hand again. "I've meant to say this before," he said hesitantly, "but it just never seemed to be the right time." He took a deep breath. "I love you, Shannon Duncan, and I want to spend the rest of my life waking up beside you."

Tears stung her eyes, and she blinked them back. "I love you too, Sam, and waking up beside you every morning would be wonderful."

He bent and kissed her lips. "You've just made me the happiest man in the world," he said. "Now go back to sleep before Nurse Ratched comes back in here and gives us both a shot of something to put us out." He used the call button to turn off the light over her bed and padded back to the couch in his bare feet.

Shannon didn't want to sleep now. Had he really just said the L-word? Had she? What did that mean with everything that had been going on? He said the Feds were involved now. Did that mean she'd be under investigation for shooting the men who'd attacked her? Sam hadn't mentioned anything about that, and she was afraid to ask.

"Are they going to arrest me for shooting those men in the cabin?" Shannon asked softly into the dark room.

"Of course not," Sam shot back. "It was self-defense, and everyone with any sense knows that."

Shannon made a soft snorting sound. "We're talking about the Feds here, you know." She grunted when she tried to move again. "I don't know how I'm gonna get around to feed my chickens and tend my garden with this hip," she said with a sigh. "Is someone making certain they're getting fed and collecting the eggs?"

"Emily said she'd come over and look after the chickens if

she could have a few fresh eggs," Sam told her with a soft chuckle, "and Teddy will keep the weeds out of your garden if he can have some tomatoes when they're ready."

Shannon rolled her eyes. "It's November, and there's nothing left of the garden for Teddy to worry about."

"There will be when we get that greenhouse finished," Sam said.

"I can't wait to see it, baby, but I can't expect other people to look after my things," Shannon said with a deep sigh. "I'll get used to this, and I suppose the pain will pass as I use it more," she said, hoping it was true because the persistent throbbing and aching was almost more than she could handle here in the hospital bed.

"Stop being silly, Shannon, someone shot you, and you've had surgery, so let us help you to put things back together," Sam said with insistence in his voice that gave her a feeling that everything was going to be all right again. She allowed sleep to take her away again to that place without pain or worry.

Unfortunately, the worry returned the following morning when agents from the Federal Bureau of Indian Affairs arrived in her room just after Sam had gone to work on her cabin with his crew.

"Good morning, Mrs. Duncan, I'm Agent Howard, and this is Agent Campbell," one of the men in suits said as Shannon pushed her tray of powdered eggs and mushy fruit aside. "We're here to speak with you about what happened at your home the other night."

Shannon studied the two men. One was younger and seemed to defer to the older one. Their suits were probably off the rack at JC Penny but fit well and were neat with contrasting ties.

"Do I need my attorney here?" Shannon asked, wondering if her attorney of record even handled cases like this, whatever this was.

The younger agent spoke up then. "You're welcome to have your attorney here, ma'am, but this is just an interview, not an interrogation, and you're not in custody for any reason."

" All right," she said with a sigh. "What do you want to know?"

"Are you familiar with Malcolm Tagert and William Gray Wolf? Have you had dealings with them in the past that might have caused animosity between yourself and them?" the older agent asked. "I believe they were known drug offenders who peddled their trash on the reservation. Were you buying drugs from them? Owed them money for drugs you hadn't paid for?"

"I haven't used drugs recreationally in decades," Shannon snapped, "and I don't know those men other than that they've vandalized my property before at the behest of Nathan Tyler and his band of goons from the reservation he calls The Brethren."

The younger man scribbled something in a notepad. "Are you saying these men were a part of a gang on the reservation?"

Shannon flinched when she tried to move. "I don't think they see themselves as a gang so much but a brotherhood on the reservation, trying to make things better for their people there."

"Selling drugs and tormenting people?" the older agent said. "We've heard of this Brethren group, and they sound like they've been organized to intimidate individuals who don't want to go along with this Nathan Tyler character and pay his extortion."

Shannon nodded. "Nathan says all the right things about Red Pride and having respect for the native population on the reservation, but as far as I can see, he's just another hustler in it for what he can get for himself out of it. He sent that big guy in his pickup to my place more than once and crashed through my gate, knocked down my planter boxes, and dumped burlap sacks filled with snakes on my patio." She took a breath. "Sam says he's a scammer and a schemer out for himself and nobody else."

"You were involved in a civil dispute with the tribe, were you not?" the young agent asked as he continued to take notes.

Emily walked in with her tray of syringes and sat them on the bed, edging the older agent away from the bed. "I need to draw some blood from this patient, gentlemen. Would you be so kind as to step out into the hall for just a minute?"

"We're Federal Agents conducting an investigation, Missy," the older agent snarled. "Come back later when we're finished."

Emily turned on the man with her eyes narrowed and her hackles up. "You assholes might be able to come on the reservation in your shiny cars and cheap suits to boss people around, but in this hospital, people like me give the orders." She pointed to the door and stormed, "and I'm telling you to get out of this room until I'm finished drawing blood from this patient."

The older agent opened his mouth to say something, but the younger man took his arm. "Just let us know when you're finished, ma'am," he said as he led the other man from the room.

"Damn," Shannon said with a soft chuckle, "remind me never to piss you off, Emily."

Emily grinned. "I hope I wasn't too rude, but men like them have been intimidating people like me on that reservation for over a hundred years, and it felt good to give a little of it back to them." She prepped Shannon's arm for the blood draw. "A little stick now," she said, and Shannon felt the needle go into her arm.

"Hey," she said with a smile, "give the asshats hell for all I care. They're probably going to arrest me and put me in cuffs anyhow."

Emily finished drawing the blood and applied another cotton ball with tape to her arm. "You don't think they'd arrest you for defending yourself in your own home, do you?"

Shannon shrugged. "I have no idea, but it sounded like they thought I was a drug customer or something and shot them in a drug deal gone wrong."

Emily shook her head and then called the men back into the room. "Look, you guys," she said, "I've known Malcolm Tagert and Will Gray Wolf all my life, and they were both bad news. Malcolm drove that truck of his around the reservation like he owned the place after Nathan made him his right-hand man. But he was just a thug who liked to rape women and make them do whatever he wanted them to do." She glanced up at Shannon. "In my opinion, this woman did a service to the community by blowing those assholes away, and someone should pin a medal on her chest, not throw her in jail." She picked up her tray and left the room without saying another word.

"Nobody is going to throw you in jail, Mrs. Duncan," Agent Howard said. "It was a clear case of self-defense on your part, and our investigation has verified what the young lady just said. Malcolm Tagert and his friend were classic bad news, and you're lucky you didn't end up with worse than a bullet in your hip."

Shannon smiled. "I think my poor house got the worst of it."

Agent Campbell nodded. "I think you're right there. I hope you have good insurance."

Shannon rolled her eyes. "After having to replace my gate twice and my chicken coop, I think I'll just bypass the insurance company and pay for this one out of my pocket. And I'm sorta glad I'm in here and don't have to see it like that."

Agent Campbell nodded. "I can certainly understand that."

"I think we have everything we need here, Mrs. Duncan," Agent Howard said. "Have a good day, and we hope you recover soon."

They left the room, and Shannon rang for the nurse to ask for a pain shot. The throbbing in her hip had changed to a constant stabbing sensation, and she was extremely uncomfortable. She slept off and on, and the doctor came in to check her wound, ask her about her pain, and give new orders to the nurse.

As they were serving lunch, Jonas Graywolf walked into her room in full reservation police uniform and a scowl on his face. "Well, it seems the Feds have let you off the hook for murdering my cousins Malcolm and Will, whore," Jonas snarled at her, "but this isn't over by a long shot, and I'm gonna be watching you over there on the property you stole from my people, and I'll see you in jail yet."

"I beg to differ, sir," Shannon said with her voice trembling. "I purchased that property legally from the previous owner. I didn't steal anything from your people or anyone else, I have the court ruling to prove it, and I didn't murder anyone."

Jonas snorted. "I don't recognize papers issued in a white man's court, whore. As far as The Brethren and I are concerned, you're trespassing on sacred tribal land, and you need to go."

"That's my land, and I'm not going anywhere, Deputy Dawg, so get out of my room and let me enjoy my lunch in peace."

He marched up and used his arm to sweep the tray of food onto the floor. "I'm an officer of the law, bitch, and you can't order me around the way you order your bunch of apples who do your bidding for what you have to offer them between your legs." He lunged at her, and Shannon tried to get away from him but couldn't because of the pain in her hip when she tried to move.

The noise of the crashing tray and their raised voices attracted the nurses' attention, and two of them rushed in as Jonas reached for Shannon's throat. "What in the name of heaven is going on in here?" one of the women screamed and yelled for the other woman to call security. "Sir, I'm going to have to ask you to leave now," she said, collecting herself.

Jonas moved away from Shannon. "This is far from over, whore, mark my words."

When Sam arrived in new clothes, the nurse pulled him aside and told him what happened with Jonas. "Are you all right, Shannon?" he asked as he took her into his arms, and she broke down sobbing with relief.

"I'm just so glad you're here, Sam, and I want to go home." She glanced up at the nurse who'd followed Sam into the room. "I think I'd feel safer there."

"The nurse said he put his hands on you," Sam said angrily, "and that your wound opened up again."

"He was mad because the Feds called it self-defense and not murder," Shannon sobbed. "My wound opened up when I was trying to get away from him on the bed. I guess I twisted wrong, and it pulled out the stitches."

"Well, you're obviously not safe here," he snarled, "so let's get you dressed and get the hell out of here."

Shannon began to weep with joy. "Oh, thank you, baby. I just want to go home and sleep with you in my own bed."

"You're probably right about her not being safe in here," the nurse who'd been standing at the door during their conversation said, "but I can't let her go without the doctor's OK first. Her surgical incision was just re-sutured this afternoon, and we have her on IV antibiotics to guard against infection. She needs to stay here for at least one more day until you finish with it." She glanced at Shannon's tear-streaked face and frowned. "I'll call the doctor to see when we can safely release you and explain the things that went on here today with that awful man and his threats." The nurse walked back toward her station as a call bell sounded in the distance.

"Jonas threatened you?" Sam demanded. "What did he say?"

"He just said this wasn't over," Shannon told him through her tears.

Sam's face turned dark. "It's going to be over now. I'm going to punch that bastard's nose so far in he's going to be blowing his belly button when he has a cold."

Shannon wrapped her arms around his neck. "Please don't do anything stupid on my account. I love you but don't want to do conjugal visits in the county jail."

Sam kissed her and laughed. "I don't even think they have the facilities for that there but thanks for the consideration."

❦ 17 ❧

Shannon's homecoming was a brilliant affair with a barbecue on the patio and friends she didn't even know she had. Teddy and Micah were there with their wives and children and Emily from the hospital, and her husband Les with their new twin babies. It was early December, but the daytime temperatures had been up into the sixties with the bright Arizona sun shining, and someone had built a blazing fire in the patio's firepit.

"Hope you don't mind a little company today," Sam said as he brought the pickup to a halt in front of her cabin, "But everybody wanted to welcome you home, and the girls thought they should do it up right now that most of the work is done here now."

Shannon glanced down at the hospital gown she'd worn home and then to the crowd of people beneath the awning. "I'm not exactly dressed for a party today."

"Well, let's get you inside and see what we can do about that." Sam helped her out of the truck and assisted her through the French doors into her bedroom with the smoke from the grill laden with burgers and chicken stinging her eyes. She smiled when someone put a cold bottle of Bud in her hand.

Shannon stared around the freshly painted bedroom and tried to find the spots where bullets had marred the drywall, but Sam and his crew had done a wonderful job of patching them, and she could only see her frilly, feminine room. "It's really good to be home," she said as she went to the closet to find something to wear and settled on a loose-fitting summer dress made of gauze in soft pastel colors. It wasn't anything fancy, but it suited the occasion and was comfortable.

Sam helped her slip it over her head and pull it down over her injured hip. Then she ran a brush through her hair and topped her head with a floppy summer hat she hoped would help hide the fact her hair needed a trim. After relieving her bladder, Shannon took a deep breath and reached for the doorknob to open the door into the living room.

"Where are you going?" Sam asked, "The party's out front."

"I know," she said through trembling lips, "but I need to see in there where it happened and make sure there are no bodies on the floor, including mine."

Sam opened the door, and Shannon walked into a neat and tidy living room with a new flat-screen television on the wall and a taxidermized white buffalo head above the Fireplace where the head of the large brown buffalo had once hung. This replacement was striking and white. She grinned at Sam. "Who did the decorating Grizzly Adams?" she asked with a chuckle.

His face paled. "If you don't like it, you can change it, of course, but the bullets shredded the head of your old buffalo, and I saw this guy down at that antique store you like and thought it would make a great addition to the place and replace the one you lost." He glanced around the room with a frown on his handsome face. "I'm afraid I don't know much about art, so you're gonna have to be the one who replaces the paintings that were trashed."

Shannon stared at the floor, where she remembered the bodies of the men she'd shot had fallen. Her stomach somersaulted, and she ran to the kitchen sink to vomit.

"Are you all right, Shannon?" Sam asked as he rushed to her side and took her hand. "Maybe having all these people here was too much with everything else," he said with a sigh. "I'm sorry. I'll ask them all to go."

Shannon stopped him. "Don't be silly," she said with a hand on his arm. "I just needed to get my bearings. I'll be fine in a minute or two. Now give me that beer so I can get the taste of that horrid hospital breakfast I just regurgitated out of my mouth."

She turned on the faucet and washed the mess from the sink while Sam went to the bedroom to find the beer. She glanced around the kitchen and saw her cabinets had been replaced as well as her stainless steel refrigerator. She smiled when her eyes lit on the new stove. A reproduction black iron cook stove with heavy iron grates over the gas burners stood where her previous model had been. It was one she'd lusted after at Home Depot but refused to purchase because of the ridiculous sale price.

"I had to replace the appliances," Sam said as he put the bottle of beer in her hand, "so Teddy said we should get the ones you wanted in the first place since the insurance was paying for it all."

Shannon gulped down a swallow of the cold brew and then kissed him hard. "I owe Teddy one of those then," she said with a grin, "because everything looks perfect."

Sam smiled. "Don't do it in front of Wendy, though," he warned, "because that girl has a jealous streak a mile wide and would probably kick your skinny white ass all the way back down to the valley."

Shannon took another drink of her beer as they walked

outside to join the rest of the party, where people were dancing to Stevie Ray Vaughan, laughing with their children, and having a generally good time in the warm Arizona sunshine.

"Well, finally," Teddy called out. "I think you should recruit her for the Sheriff's Department, Les, because she did more in one night to clean the scum from Apache County than you guys have done in like forever."

Les raised his beer in a toast. "Indeed, she did, and took a bullet for her trouble as well, so we just might have to make her an honorary member of the force for her contribution and sacrifice."

Shannon felt her cheeks beginning to burn with embarrassment. "Don't you guys have to meet with a department shrink after you shoot someone in the line of duty?" she teased as Les nodded, "Because I think they'd probably disqualify me for service," she said as she twirled her finger over her temple and crossed her eyes.

She walked up to Teddy, wrapped her arms around his neck, and planted a sloppy kiss on his cheek while his wife Wendy looked on with a grin on her pretty face. "I told you she was gonna like that stove."

"Isn't it beautiful?" Shannon said, "and it's perfect for a country cabin like this."

"I hope the buffalo wasn't going too far, but Sam insisted you'd love him," Wendy added. "And he wanted to replace your other one."

"I do love him," Shannon said as she sat, and someone put a plate of food in front of her. "He goes perfect with the pottery, and the white buffalo is supposed to be good luck. Lord knows I could use some of that," Shannon grinned at the assembled group. "Everything is back to the way I wanted it before that terrible night with all that mess, and I thank you all for the hard work you put into it to make it happen before I got home."

"Don't thank us," Micah called out from beside his wife and young son, "it was all Sam. He even cleaned up all the blood himself, and that pig Malcolm made on hell if a mess with his blood all over the floor." He grinned and spread his arms wide.

His wife Cassie smacked on Micah's shoulder when she saw the look of horror on Shannon's face. "You should just ignore his drunk Indian mouth, Shannon," Cassie said. "He doesn't know when to keep it shut half the time."

"What'd I say?" Micah asked with his face twisted in confusion. "Malcolm bled like a stuck hog, and Sam had to clean it all up off the floor. Will didn't bleed half that much, and neither did Shannon."

Shannon squeezed her eyes shut. If he'd bled out, that meant he'd been alive for some time after she'd shot him and probably suffered before he died. He'd tried to kill her, but Shannon couldn't bear the thought of having made the man suffer before he'd finally died. She got up from the table and hurried into the cabin with everyone's eyes on her back.

"You're a damned idiot, Micah," Cassie said after delivering another slap to her husband's shoulder. "The woman didn't need to hear that shit. She just got home from the damned hospital and didn't need to hear about the blood left behind on her floor."

Sam followed Shannon into the cabin and put his arms around her trembling shoulders. "Are you all right, baby?"

"Yeah," she said with a deep sigh as she stood over the deep farm sink, staring down at the drain, "it just bothered me a little to hear that asshat probably suffered before he died."

"That asshat got just what he deserved, Shan, and don't you give it any more thought."

Shannon turned and snuggled into Sam's arms. "I'm glad you're here, Sam."

He snorted out a little laugh as he hugged her closer. "It's not like I have anywhere else to go," he said. "Nathan and his

Brethren saw to that. Les said Sylvia wouldn't let them in her shack to search for my furniture and appliances before Graywolf showed up to chase them off the reservation."

Shannon pushed back and stared up at Sam. "Don't they have to honor a warrant even on the reservation?"

"Les said they'd have to get with the Federal Agents to enforce it," Sam said with a shrug, "But I don't know if it's even worth it at this point."

Shannon shook her head. "I can't believe your mother stole from you and then burned down your house."

Sam smiled. "It was likely more Nathan and his Brethren scum than Sylvia, but I'm sure she was glad to have the things in that dump of hers on the reservation to keep Nathan happy."

"Well, you know you're welcome to stay here for as long as you'd like," Shannon told him with a kiss. as she glanced out the window, and thunder boomed in the distance. "It sounds as though our lovely weather is about to change. Let's get everyone inside before it starts to rain."

Sam shrugged. "It's that time of the year. We'll be lucky if it doesn't turn to snow before the night is over and the temperature drops." He went to the door and called everyone inside. "Get in here before this turns to snow," he called as the first fat drops of rain began to pelt the flagstone on the patio.

Micah went to Shannon's side and took her hand. "I'm so sorry to have upset you, Miss Shannon."

She hugged him. "It's all right, Micah. I shouldn't be so sensitive."

Cassie joined them. "This place is so awesome," she said. "I'd never have thought you could make such a nice home from what is essentially a storage shed."

Shannon grinned. "Well, technically, it's two," she said, glancing at the bedroom section, "but it's perfect for just one person like me." She smiled in Sam's direction. "Well, or maybe two."

Teddy smiled, joining them. "Do you two have something to tell us?"

Sam glanced at Shannon. "I guess I'll be moving in here since I don't have an address of my own for the time being."

Wendy wandered around the living room, studying her pieces of artwork on the walls. "Did you do these, Shannon? They're beautiful."

Shannon smiled. "Most of them," she said, "but I picked up a few of 'em at art sales and antique stores too."

"You have a great eye," Wendy said. "I bet you could set up at the fair and sell your stuff if you wanted to."

Shannon rolled her eyes. "Someone told me a long time ago that I was destined to be a starving artist if I continued down that path," she said with a giggle.

Wendy studied the shredded canvas of an elk. "I bet this one looked awesome in here."

"It did," Teddy said. "It's a shame those assholes trashed it with their stupid guns."

"I can paint another one," Shannon sail hesitantly. "I still have the sketches I did for the original and can redo it the next time I'm feeling in the mood."

"Well, I don't know what you charge for your work, but I'd love some of your pieces."

"And I'd like one of these cabins," Cassie said. "We can put it on that piece of land mom and dad have up by Vernon."

Micah grinned and winked at Sam. "We could always get a piece of land on the reservation."

Cassie snorted. "Those old bastards don't want you or me on their damned reservation, hon, so we'd better stick with the land up by Vernon."

Sam chuckled. "She's got you there, Micah. Vernon's not so bad, and it's a lot closer to Show Low and shopping than the reservation."

"I've got no desire to be anywhere I'm not wanted," Micah snarled. "Those greedy assholes can keep their damned casino checks. We don't need their charity." He hugged his wife. "To hell with all their new Tribal Laws. We don't need it or them."

"Do you plan to teach your children the Zuni ways?" Shannon asked.

Micah nodded. "My children have two fine Zuni uncles to teach them the Zuni ways," he said, "and their aunt Shannon lives on the ceremonial dance grounds where they can learn all the old dances and stories they need to know."

"Yeah," Sam said with a sigh, "I think the dance grounds are only gonna be open to certain people by special invitation from here on out."

Shannon rolled her eyes. "Do you really think that's a good idea, Sweetheart? I don't want to bring about any more hard feelings than there already are about this."

"Sam is right," Emily said, speaking up for the first time. "They've claimed Tribal Law to boot all of us here off the rolls of the tribe. They deserve no consideration in my way of thinking, and they tried to kill Shannon, for Christ's sake." She shook her head. "Is anybody going to pay for Sam's burned down house?"

"Not likely since Jonas won't allow any investigators on the reservation to interrogate Nathan and Sylvia."

Teddy grinned. "I say we fight fire with fire and burn down that old bitch's house on the res." He did a parody of striking a match, and everyone laughed.

"Oh no," Sam protested, "because if I know my sweet mother, she'd be over here trying to move in with us, and I need that shit like I need another hole in my damned head."

Before dusk, the rain changed to snow, and by the time people began leaving for home, an inch of the white stuff had accumulated on their trucks and cars.

Wendy hugged Shannon before stepping from beneath the covered patio. "I can't wait to see what you do with this place for Christmas. I bet it will be spectacular."

"The ex got custody of all my antique Christmas decorations," Shannon said with a sigh, "so I'm gonna have to start over here from scratch."

"I'm sure it will be beautiful whatever you do," Teddy said as he whisked his wife toward their truck with their sleeping son on his shoulder.

❦ 18 ❧

Three weeks after arriving home from the hospital and two weeks after Thanksgiving—a holiday that went unrecognized in the native communities, Shannon placed an antique glass star ornament she'd found in an antique store on the top of the freshly cut spruce. She and Sam had cut the tree themselves at a local Christmas Tree farm that afternoon and had fun doing it together.

The cabin still smelled of the popcorn they'd popped to string with cranberries as a garland, and the floor was littered with the boxes candy canes had come in. Shannon had decided this tree would be decorated in the theme of her western settler motif, and she was sticking to it over Sam's protests. Twinkling modern lights draped the branches—her only concession— hung along with the antique glass ornaments, silver tensile, and gingerbread cookies Shannon had baked and fought Sam to protect.

"If you don't stop eating my gingerbread men," she'd lovingly teased that afternoon, "there won't be any left to go on the tree."

"Then you shouldn't have made them taste so good," he said as he bit the head off another cookie and grinned.

"I'm gonna replace those with ones made from sawdust and rubber cement," she snarled.

He grinned. "Just like the ones Mother used to make."

Shannon stepped down from the ladder and frowned. "Don't you dare bring up that horrible woman in my house, Sam."

Someone knocked on the door, and Shannon shook her head as she moved around Sam and motioned for him to pick up some of the mess from the floor. Her breath caught in her throat when she got a look at the native man standing outside on her porch. He was the spitting image of Sam, but older.

"May I help you?" Shannon stuttered as she tried to imagine who this could be. Hadn't Sam told her his father had been lost in Vietnam? Perhaps this was an uncle or older cousin.

"I'm looking for Samuel Sweetwater," the man said cordially, "and was told this was where he resides now."

"It is," Shannon said. "Won't you come in?" She offered her hand. "I'm Shannon Duncan."

He took her hand. "Samuel Broken Feather," he said as he stepped through the door.

"You have a visitor, Sam," Shannon said.

Sam turned away from the Christmas tree with a ginger-bread cookie half in his mouth, and his eyes went wide at the sight of the man beside Shannon. "Damn," was all he could seem to say, and he repeated it several times before dropping into one of the leather club chairs in front of the fireplace. "I thought you were dead, Samuel Broken Feather."

The older man smiled. "I came close to it more times than I care to think on," he said as he walked over and offered his hand to his son, "but I'm finally free and back home with my people where I belong."

"Sylvia said you were captured and held prisoner in Vietnam?"

The old man grinned. "Yeah, but those bamboo cages

couldn't hold a Zuni warrior, and I escaped until the Viet Cong finally got tired of me and sent me off to China where they tried to reeducate me and turn me into a double agent for their side."

"You've been in a Chinese prison all this time?" Shannon gasped. "That's unfathomable."

"I thought everybody had forgotten about me over here," he said, "but evidently my brother's daughter started a letter-writing campaign on my behalf after I wasn't released with the other Vietnam POWs and the Chinese finally did a prisoner exchange with me, and here I am."

"What do you plan to do with yourself now that you're home?" Sam asked.

The older man shrugged. "Apply for Social Security, I suppose, and try to find all my family who's still alive."

"There are still Broken Feathers on the Reservation," Sam said, "but your mom passed some years back and your brother Evan after he got out of prison."

Sam's father shook his head. "Evan spent most of his life behind bars because he couldn't control his urges for drink and drugs while I spent most of my life behind bars because I was a soldier fighting for my country."

"And is your country going to recognize you for that sacrifice?" Shannon asked.

Samuel Broken Feather shrugged his shoulders. "My VA Rep said something about lunch at the White House with whoever it is who's President now, but he warned me to avoid the press, or it could jeopardize me financially."

"Where are you staying?" Sam asked.

"They put me up in the Best Western in Snowflake," he said with a grin. "Even gave me chits for food in the restaurant or room service."

"Have you seen Sylvia?" Sam asked hesitantly with a glance at Shannon.

"I walked by her old house on the reservation and saw her

and some guy out in the yard," he said, "so I didn't stop. Is he the man who raised you in my place, Samuel? I'm proud she at least gave you my first name if not Broken Feather as she should have."

Sam cleared his throat. "Broken Feather wasn't her name to give me," he said in a scolding tone. "It was yours or your mother's."

"I wrote to both your mother and mine after I got the letter from Sylvi, telling me she carried you in her womb after we'd," he coughed nervously, "well, after we did what we'd done before I left for Vietnam," the older man said, "and told them to give the baby my name when it was born, but I don't know why that didn't happen."

Sam shrugged his shoulders. "Sylvia said there was bad blood between the Sweetwaters and the Broken Feathers, and your mother wouldn't give her permission to bestow the good Broken Feather name on the bastard baby of a Sweetwater tramp, who'd likely spread her legs for every boy on the reservation, hoping to trap one in a good marriage or your case, the benefits from the military."

Samuel Broken Feather shook his head. "My mother could be a stubborn old squaw when she wanted to be, and those checks I sent home every month were her only income at the time, so I suspect she guarded them with her life." He frowned. "But I knew I was Sylvia's first when I took her that night and told my mother before I left for Vietnam that if she showed up with a baby in her belly that it was mine and to treat her and you with respect. I don't know why she didn't."

"Probably those monthly checks," Shannon said with a sigh. "How long did they continue after the Viet Cong captured you?"

"Until I was declared dead, I think," Samuel said. "They would have sent her a check for eighty percent of my earnings even after they captured me from what I understand."

"Then she was getting them well into the eighties until the

congress declared all the missing in action from the war dead," Shannon said.

Samuel Broken Feather stared at his son, and Shannon wondered if the older man saw a shadow of himself in his son. "It was still no reason for her to deny you as mine when you obviously are. I'm a half-blind old man, but I can see you are the image of me in my younger days." He ran a hand over his close-cropped hair. "The Chinese shave the heads of their prisoners," he said nervously, "but it's growing back." He smiled at Sam. "I'm glad to see you keep our traditions though I wasn't here to teach them to you as a father should."

Samuel stared around the festively decorated cabin. "Do I, by chance, have grandchildren I might teach the old ways to?"

Sam shook his head. "I regret I was never blessed with children. My first wife divorced me, and my second was killed in an accident before our child could be born."

Shannon's breath caught in her throat. Why didn't she know that his wife had been pregnant when she died?

"And this wife?" Samuel asked cordially.

Shannon saw the flash of embarrassment on Sam's face, and she answered in his place. "Not his wife," she said with a grin, "and this body is much too old to carry a baby. I'm afraid the plumbing dried up some time ago."

At their age, the topic of a child resulting from their love-making had never come up. Did he want a child? Shannon thought they would be having a long discussion before they slept tonight.

She heard the timer on the oven sound, and she stood. "I have a pot roast with all the fixin's in the oven, Mr. Broken Feather. Will you join Sam and me for supper?"

He smiled, and Shannon noted again that he was in serious need of dental work. "I'd be honored, but my ride will be back in half an hour," he said, "and please call me Samuel. Mr. Broken Feather was my grandfather, and he was a mean old drunk I've spent the last sixty years or so trying to forget."

Sam glanced at Shannon to get an idea if she'd caught the same thing in what Samuel had just said. "Does that mean your mother wasn't married, either, and your father didn't raise you?" Sam asked, suddenly furious at the Broken Feathers for their insults about his mother and him.

Samuel shook his gray head. "My mother's father was a bad man," he said, "and drank worse than my brother." He took a deep breath before continuing. "One night, when he'd been drinking hard, I walked into my mother's room and found him on her in the bed. I tried to pull him off her, and he sat up laughing and told me to get out and let him finish so he could make a little brother or sister for me." The old man hung his head in shame. "My grandfather was also my father." He sighed. "I'd reckon that or a night close to it was when my brother Evan was conceived."

"There's no shame in that for you," Shannon said as she rose to go to the oven and tend to her roast. "You had no say in who your father was or how you came about."

"I've told myself that all my life," Samuel said, "but every time I looked at that old man, I saw him on my mother and just wanted to throw up."

Shannon put the meal on the table and called the men in to eat. Before they'd finished, they heard a loud knocking on the door, and Shannon got up to answer it, suspecting it was Samuel's ride back to Snowflake. She opened the door to an attractive native woman around her age. "I'm here for my Uncle Samuel," she said in a sour clipped tone that told Shannon the woman hadn't wanted him to make this visit.

"Please come in," Shannon said, "he's just finishing up supper."

The woman lifted a brow. "I made dinner for him at home," she said.

"I'm sorry," Shannon said. "I had a roast in the oven and thought it would be rude not to offer to share it with him."

The woman pushed past Shannon and went into the

kitchen. "I don't suppose you could have left the roast in the oven until I'd picked him up."

"You should marry that woman, son," Shannon heard Samuel say, "because I haven't eaten a meal this good since I got back home."

"Is that so, Uncle?" the woman said in a hurt tone.

Oh, hi, Melody," Samuel said. "This nice lady here invited me to break bread with her and my son, so I couldn't say no. It wouldn't have been the honorable thing to do."

Melody snorted. "These two have no honor, Uncle. Don't you recognize where she built this house where she now shacks up with a red man like a common whore?" She grinned at Sam. But you'd be used to that, wouldn't you, Sam? Your mother got you used to living with a whore, didn't she?"

Melody Broken Feather, apologize to this woman and your cousin," Samuel snapped.

"I've got nothing to apologize for, Uncle," Melody replied. "Sylvia Sweetwater is a whore. Your mother told us she was and that Sam couldn't be your son because you'd already left for Vietnam when she got herself pregnant."

Samuel shook his head, and then he looked up at Shannon. "I must apologize for my misinformed niece then." He turned to his niece. "My mother knew Sylvia might be pregnant with my child before I left for Vietnam and denied him so she wouldn't have to share my benefit checks with her." He stood and glared at his niece. "At this point, I'm disgusted by the Broken Feather women." He turned back to Sam. "Will you give this old man a ride back to his hotel in Snowflake, son?" Then he turned to Melody again. "He is my son, Melody, and if you look at him close even your jaded eyes, you should see the resemblance between us."

Melody snorted. "He could be the get of my daddy or even Grandpa. Grandma said she was a little slut who'd spread her legs for any man who might give her a way off the reservation."

It was time for Samuel to snort. "Your grandfather would have been more likely to crawl into your bed to take his pleasure than look for it from a girl on the street."

Melody's face drained of color. "What are you saying, Uncle?"

"What I'm saying, niece, is that your grandfather was a lecherous old drunk who liked to pleasure himself in the beds of his daughters."

Melody's mouth dropped open. "You mean?"

"Yes, I mean my father was also my grandfather, as was he your father's."

"Oh, my god," Melody gasped as she sprang to her feet. "You're such a liar, and I'm sorry I spent so much of my time organizing a letter-writing campaign to find you and bring you home." She turned to leave and then turned back with tears streaming down her face. Nathan is right about the lot of you here, and none of you deserve to be called Zuni." She stormed out, slamming the door behind her.

"Wow," Shannon said as she sopped up the last of the gravy on her plate with a biscuit.

Samuel smiled. "Well, I don't figure you'd be expecting to be called Zuni, would you, young lady?"

"No," Shannon said, "and they've kicked Sam off the rolls now, so you're the only official Zuni here."

Samuel's mouth dropped open, and he turned to his son. "What is she talking about, son?"

Sam shrugged. "Sylvia and her white-hating man friend, Nathan Tyler, had me dropped from the tribal rolls because of my relationship with Shannon and their greed for bigger cuts of those casino earnings."

"The Tyler who is running for tribal governor?" Samuel asked as he shook his head. "I can't believe the greed of my people today."

❦ 19 ❦

Shannon and Sam sat with Samuel as they watched the election results for the Zuni governorship on a local station.

"It looks like this Tyler is going to win the election," Samuel said.

"More's the pity for the Zuni tribe," Sam said.

"Well, I guess Sylvia will be able to move off the reservation if the governor has a nice residence at the Pueblo," Shannon said with a wink at Sam. "Maybe you can recover your missing furniture and appliances."

Sam shrugged. "I have no place to put them now."

She smiled at Samuel. "Oh, I don't know about that," she said.

He stared at her for a minute and then his father. "All right, what are the two of you up to?"

"Well, boy," Samuel said hesitantly, clearing his throat, "the VA is gonna boot me out of that nice hotel now that the hoopla is all over with the President and the news crews have stopped coming around." He shrugged. "This sweet lady of yours has offered me a piece of her land here, and we're going to put one of these nice cabins on it. She's going to lend this old man the money until he gets his promised back pay from Uncle Sam."

Sam glanced at Shannon, and she nodded. "There's plenty of room out here for a second cabin," she said, "and having Samuel here when you're off working would be nice."

Sam frowned for a minute. "The only other nice flat spot is the dance grounds," he said. "Do we want to kick that hornet's nest?"

The television erupted with loud applause as it switched from a crime drama to the Zuni governor race to announce that Nathan Tyler had just won. He stood on a podium with Sylvia at his side, glowing with the applause. With a broad smile on his face, Nathan brought her hand to his lips and kissed it.

"Your mother is still the blooming flower I remember," Samuel said as he stared at Sylvia's image on the screen. "I wonder if she even remembers me."

Sam reached into his shirt pocket and removed the faded Polaroid Sylvia had given him. He handed it to his father. "Oh, she remembers you all right. She carried this for almost sixty years."

Samuel studied the old photo, and tears brimmed in his eyes. "That was a proud day for me," he said, "and the day you were conceived, I'd reckon," he added with a shy grin.

Nathan cleared his throat and began to speak. "I'm honored to accept this esteemed position as the Governor of my people," he began. " The Zuni are a fine, strong people who deserve a strong leader at this time of change in our society." There was first cheering and applause, and then the crowd quieted to listen to what Sam knew would be more of Nathan and his mother's racist bullshit.

"And here it comes," Sam groaned as Nathan continued.

"We hear every day how Black lives matter," Nathan boomed, "and they do, but Red lives matter as well, and it's time for our voices to be heard." The crowd cheered wildly, and Nathan waited for them to quiet until he went on. "For too long, the white man has dominated us, but with our casinos, we've taken the white man by the short hairs and given him his comeuppance." This brought about more cheering. "We will build more casinos on Tribal Lands and suck what the white man cares about most from his hands—his money." More wild cheering from the crowd. "But Tribal Laws must also be changed to reflect how the white man has tried to overcome us on our reservations. He's tried to corrupt our blood with his, and it's time for us to put a stop to that." There was more cheering, but they noted it wasn't as fervent as before. "It's time for we Zuni to be the first to enact Tribal Laws to protect our bloodlines from being polluted and weakened by white blood. We must strip all who marry or cohabitate with whites from our Tribal rolls and deny their impure children membership in the Tribe."

"It sounds like this asshat is using Mr. Hitler's Mien Kampf as a playbook," Samuel said with a stern frown.

"You have no idea," Sam said, rolling his eyes.

Shannon shook her head. "He's gonna have federal authorities crawling up his behind making statements like that on television."

Samuel turned to his son. "Does your mother buy into that racist propaganda?"

"Hook, line, and sinker, I'm afraid," Sam said with a nod.

"Then I don't suppose she'll be your matron of honor at the wedding," Samuel said with a chuckle.

"Wedding?" Sam said with his brow furrowed. "What wedding?"

Samuel winked at Shannon. "Your wedding to this daughter of my heart," he said.

"Thanks for spoiling my surprise, Dad," Sam said in mock anger as he got to his knees before Shannon and fished in his pocket for something. "Shannon Duncan," he said in a formal tone, "would you consider doing this red man the honor of becoming his wife?" He took her hand and slipped a silver ring studded with turquoise and garnets onto her finger.

Tears filled her eyes as she stared at the beautiful ring she knew had been crafted by Doc. "Of course I will, you silly man. I love you."

They kissed as Samuel sat with a satisfied grin on his weathered face. "When you plan the wedding feast, keep in mind that I like those little weenies wrapped in dough you dip in bar-b-que sauce."

Sam laughed as he held his bride-to-be in his arms. "We'll put that at the top of the list, Dad."

❦

"I think that went well," Nathan said as he and Sylvia sat in their luxury hotel room at the Pueblo Casino.

"I'm scrolling through replays on the internet now and listening to all the commentators," she said, "I think ..."

Nathan looked up from removing his shiny new boots. "You think what, my dear?" he asked when Sylvia stopped speaking. She sat staring at the computer screen, and Nathan rose to see what she was watching so intently. "What is it? You look as though you've seen a ghost."

"I think I have," Sylvia mumbled as tears filled her eyes. "Why didn't I know about this?"

On the computer screen sat Samuel Broken Feather, talking to a national correspondent about his time in Vietnam, his imprisonment in China, and his recent release in a spy trade.

"Oh," Nathan said in a dismissive tone, "I saw that piece of fluff but didn't want to bother you with it."

"Bother me with it?" Sylvia said, bolting to her feet. "You know that man is Sammy's father. How could you think I wouldn't want to know he was alive and returned to us?"

Nathan snorted. "He obviously doesn't care that much

about you or his son," Nathan sneered. "He walked right past us a few months ago and never said word one."

Sylvia's eyes went wide. "A few months ago," she mumbled. "Where?"

"Right in front of that squalid shack your son moved you into on the reservation," he snapped.

"Samuel is back on the reservation?" she gasped and began to gather her things from the hotel's bureau and throw them into her suitcase.

Nathan grabbed her arm. "What do you think you're doing, Sylvia?" he snapped. "We have commitments here at the Pueblo in the morning."

"You have commitments, Governor," Sylvia snapped as she tried to jerk her arm from his grasp, "not me. Take your white tramp with you. I'm going home."

Sylvia had assumed they would marry before the election, and Nathan had presented her as his intended bride at most functions, but Sylvia found out the hard way that the man had only been using her when she'd walked into their suite at one of the many hotels on campaign stops and found him in bed with his white press secretary.

Nathan laughed but didn't release her arm. Instead, he slapped her hard on the face. "You'll stay here, Sylvia," he sneered as tears of rage and frustration filled her eyes, "and play the part of my token red squaw, who does as she's told and knows her place." He pushed her, and Sylvia stumbled into the table where their celebratory room service meal's remains lay. "Did you really think I'd marry a dried-up old hag like you, Sylvia?" Nathan said with a deep-throated chuckle. "First, I used you for the money you got from that ingrate son of yours, and then I used you as a red woman on my arm to show the people I wasn't a race traitor like your Sam."

"I swore many years ago that no man would ever strike me

again," Sylvia hissed, "but I never expected that man to be Zuni or someone I thought I respected."

"You're an old fool, Sylvia," Nathan said with a chuckle. "You deserve to have been the way I used you. And I'll continue to use you for as long as it suits me." He laughed maniacally as he slapped her again.

Nathan Tyler, the newly elected governor of the Zuni people, laughed when the steak knife pierced his heart, and he took his last breath, staring up into the aged, grinning face of Sylvia Sweetwater. "I swore a long time ago that I'd kill the next man who laid a hand on me, Nathan," she said calmly. "Now I'm calling my son and going home."

☙❧

At the press conference held on the Zuni reservation, a weeping Sylvia Sweetwater with her son Sam and the recently returned Vietnam POW, Samuel Broken Feather at her side, accepted the position of Governor of the Zuni.

She'd told the authorities how a drunken Nathan Tyler had attacked her in their hotel room after he'd admitted to her he'd been having an affair with his press secretary and wanted her to return to the reservation after he'd been sworn in as Governor and had no intention of marrying her after all his promises. Her bruised arm, cut lip, and fractured jaw had been all the proof they needed to call the killing of Governor-elect Nathan Tyler justifiable homicide.

When she went before the Zuni Council of Elders, they were happy to offer her the governorship when she replayed all the campaign videos to show her involvement and the people's cheering when she spoke about the issues closest to her heart and the rebuilding of the Zuni people.

"Madam Sweetwater," one elder said, "while we appreciate the zeal with which Mr. Tyler approached this office, it worries us that you too might take the same stand as he

concerning thinning the rolls of our tribe with racially moti-
vated laws."

Sylvia frowned. "Mr. Tyler had the best of intentions
there," she said, "but perhaps he took his statements at the
press conference after the election a little too far. I fear he was
drunk with both alcohol and power that dreadful night."

She used the sash about her narrow waist to dab a tear
from her eye. "If you grant me the honor of replacing him as
governor, I will instill in our people that we should return to
the old ways, perform our ceremonies not to the public at the
white man's orchestrated Pow-wows, but on our sacred ceremonial sites restricted to just our people and not for public
consumption."

"I would also pursue the Federal government for more
university campuses on our reservation to encourage our
young people to be educated. Too many have been lost to the
white man's drink and drugs," she said fervently. "Too many
leave the reservation to pursue an education at the white
man's schools and return addicted to these drugs or in the case
of our young women, with a white man's baby in her belly the
tribe must accept and care for." She shook her head. "Something must be done."

When she saw scowls on some of the faces, Sylvia
returned to the topic of education. "We need textbooks
written from the native point of view in our educational insti-
tution. We need books that glorify men like Geronimo and
Sitting Bull rather than vilifying them as the white man's textbooks do while standing butchers like Custer and Crook as
heroes. It is time our children were taught the other side of
the story. I love that T-shirt they sell in the tourist traps that
shows a group of native men around a fire and says Fighting
Terrorism for Centuries Now." Sylvia smiled and giggled
softly.

That seemed to appease the Elders, and they offered her
the position as governor of the Zuni nation. She chose to hold

her swearing-in ceremony on the reservation in Apache County, Arizona, where she resided. She asked that she be allowed to make her humble home there the governor's residence during her tenure.

When Sam received the call from Sylvia about what had happened at the Pueblo, he'd hurried to her side—the joy of his engagement to Shannon pushed to the back of his mind. The three-hour drive to the Pueblo was the longest of his life, and he didn't know what he'd have done without Samuel at his side.

"She's an old woman," Sam swore. "I can't believe that dirtbag would touch her like that after everything she did to get his ass elected."

"Calm down, son," Samuel said as they finally reached the exit onto I-40. "Just breathe in the beauty of the land around you and allow it to fill you with its peace."

"I suppose you studied at a Zhou Lin temple while you were in China," Sam said with a grin.

Samuel smiled. "There are few virtues in being locked away in a solitary confinement prison," he said, " but learning to meditate and becoming one with yourself is one of them."

They drove on in silence for some time until they reached the busy Pueblo in New Mexico, where they sought out Sylvia in a different hotel room from the one where Nathan had attacked her and died. She rushed into Sam's arms when she opened the door and saw his concerned face. "Oh, Sammy, it was so horrible, and you were right about Nathan all along. All he wanted to do was use me for what he could get from me and win this election."

She sobbed on Sam's shoulder until he pulled her away. "I brought someone with me who might cheer you up some," he said as they moved into the hotel room and closed the door.

Sylvia noted Samuel's presence for the first time and hurried to brush the tears from her eyes. "Hello, Sylvy," Samuel said, offering her his hand. "It has been some years since we last saw one another, but you are still the same delicate desert flower I first laid eyes upon all those years ago."

Sam grinned. He thought that Temple must have also taught a course in slick moves. Samuel took Sylvia into his arms and held her close to him, and she slumped into the man she'd told her son was the only true love of her life. "Oh, Samuel," she wept like a schoolgirl, "I thought you were dead."

"I know, my love," Samuel cooed softly, "and I'm so sorry for leaving you alone here to raise my son alone." He smiled down at her. "But you did an amazing job. He's every bit the man I'd have wanted him to be had I been here to raise him myself."

Yep, Sam thought, the old man must have gotten high marks in that slick moves class at the temple. Sylvia ate it up, and when he went down to register them for rooms, Sylvia told him only to get one for himself because she and Samuel had decades to catch up o

❦ 20 ❦

The wedding of Sam Sweetwater and Shannon Duncan didn't occur without some bumps and bruises. Sylvia let it be known quite vociferously that she would not be attending, while Samuel went on praising Shannon whenever he had the chance, especially within Sylvia's hearing.

"I simply cannot condone this marriage, Samuel," she said again as he dressed in his ceremonial garb for the event. "and I don't see how you can either. Our son should be marrying a good Zuni woman and not that white whore."

"I've told you before, Sylvy, that I'll not have Shannon disparaged in my home."

Sylvia snorted. "Has she bought you the same way she bought our son, Samuel, with her lottery money and this shabby excuse for a cabin for you to live in on our people's sacred ceremonial grounds that she stole from us in the white man's court?"

Samuel stared around the small but comfortable space and smiled. "She's helped to give me a home on land I can consider my own," he said, "where I can grow my food, tend my livestock and finally call home. I thought I'd never have that again, Sylvy, and I can be close to the son I didn't know in the years when he needed a father's guidance."

"You should have guided him away from this race traitor marriage," was all she said before storming out of the bathroom to sit in front of the fireplace where an unneeded fire burned.

Sam and his crew had spent weeks insulating, drywalling, and finishing the cabin for Samuel. They'd also built him a chicken coop and tilled up a garden space for him behind the building that sat in a meadow on the far end of Shannon's property.

Shannon, who knew a woman in northern California with a leather shop and created amazing clothing items, had ordered a white dress made from soft lambskin decorated with an assortment of beads and fringe in place of lace. It wasn't a purely native design and not totally Victorian either, but it paid homage, she thought, to both cultures and was beautiful.

"I hope your Native friends aren't going to be offended by this dress," Shannon said to Emily as she laced the corseted ties in the back.

"I don't see why anyone would be," the young medical technician said. "I think it's beautiful and tasteful at the same time."

"I just hope Sam likes it," Shannon said as Emily helped her lace the long cuffs on the mutton sleeves.

"He hasn't seen it?" Emily said in surprise. "This thing is a work of art, and I'd be afraid to wear it for fear of spilling something on it."

Shannon smiled as she stared at her reflection in the tall, oval mirror. "It's bad luck for the groom to see the dress before the wedding day," she said, "and Sam and I certainly don't need any more bad luck."

The wedding was being held beneath the wide awning above Shannon's flagstone patio, and her raised beds were filled with fragrant summer flowers along with the vegetables.

Doc, who was also a Zuni shaman, was officiating, and two dozen chairs had been set up in the shade of the junipers dotting the yard for the few invited guests.

Invitations had been sent out to the Broken Feather family, but few had RSVP'd. Teddy, Micah, and their families would be in attendance along with Doc's daughter and a few other local individuals who did business with Sam, but Shannon expected it to be a small intimate affair. She touched up her makeup as Emily took the curlers from her hair and allowed the mass of artificial curls to fall to Shannon's shoulders.

Half an hour before the ceremony, Shannon heard Sam, Teddy, and Samuel talking quietly in the living room. "How many people did you invite, man?" Teddy asked, "because there's a line of cars outside your gate, and people are asking where to park."

"We only invited about twenty people," she heard Sam say as her gut began to wrench at the thought of trouble here on her wedding day.

"I may have mentioned it to a few of the fellas down at the VFW," Samuel said hesitantly, "but I told 'em all if they were planning to come, it would be a BYOB and potluck situation."

"Aww, Dad," she heard Sam say, "you might have mentioned that before today so we could have planned for a bigger group of people."

"It'll be fine, Son. The guys from the VFW will keep any of those rascal Brethren who are still prowling about in line if any of them show up to cause trouble."

Shannon's heart leaped in her throat at the mention of the Brethren. She didn't think they were around much since the shooting here and Nathan's death at the Pueblo, but she certainly didn't want any of them showing up at her wedding to cause trouble. This was her day, and she didn't want to have to put her 357 on over her wedding gown.

"I don't suppose our governor is planning to attend," she heard Sam ask his father.

"I've no idea," Samuel replied. "She was stomping around in the cabin when I left to walk over here. I've tried to talk to her, but you know she's a mite mule-headed."

"Tell me about it," Sam said. "I was hoping she'd change her mind and try to embrace my happiness, but I don't suppose she will."

"I know, boy," Samuel said, "and I know she'll regret it if she misses her only child's wedding, but it's her decision to make and not ours. We have to respect that."

"I know, Dad," Sam said with a deep sigh. "I know."

When Shannon placed the order for her wedding dress, she'd also ordered a three-tiered skirt and doeskin blouse for Sylvia and had it delivered to her house on the reservation, but she had no idea if she'd received it or would wear it to the wedding. Her friend had assured her the ensemble would be beaded and decorated with traditional Zuni designs, and Shannon had hoped it might be a peace offering though she doubted there would ever be peace between her and Sam's mother.

Drums began to beat outside, and Shannon gathered herself to make her exit through the French doors on the bedroom that led out onto the patio where her groom waited.

"Are you ready, Daughter of my Heart?" Samuel asked as he took Shannon by the arm to march her out to the ceremonial Zuni drums' beat. He kissed her forehead. "You are a beautiful bride," he said. "My son is a damned lucky man."

Shannon winked at her father-in-law-to-be. "I made a huge pan of those little weenies you requested, and there's a special tray just for you warming in the oven."

Samuel grinned. "Are you sure you don't want to marry me instead of my son?"

Shannon heard gasps when she stepped out in the dress with the clear, blue, and green glass beads stitched to the front, sparkling in the bright Arizona sunshine. She was shocked to see the gathered crowd's size but more surprised to see the new Zuni governor sitting resplendent in the beaded and fringed doeskin shirt and long three-tiered skirt. Her neck bent with the weight of heavy silver and turquoise squash blossom jewelry, and the cuffs of the blouse were held tight by heavy silver bracelets.

"It looks as though the governor made it after all," Shannon whispered into Sam's ear when she reached him, and his father had taken his place on his other side as his best man.

"Let's just hope she doesn't break into one of her racist rants," he said, rolling his brown eyes.

"Do I have your permission to shoot her if she does?" Shannon asked with a grin.

Sam's eyes went wide. "Tell me you're not wearing that gun under your skirt."

She just smiled and winked as Doc began the wedding ceremony. The ceremony was a mash-up of the traditional civil ceremony of the state and the Zuni. The drums continued at different rates of speed at certain times and quieted almost completely when she and Sam exchanged their vows to love, honor, and cherish one another.

Women came over to congratulate her, and Shannon thought the majority were sincere though Sylvia wasn't one of them. She'd kept her distance all afternoon, and Shannon was nervous she was going to make a scene before the evening was out.

"Your dress is quite outstanding," a female voice said from behind her, and Shannon turned to find Sylvia Sweetwater standing there with a glass of wine in her hand. "Thank you for these, by the way," she said, motioning to her clothes.

"I hoped you'd like them," Shannon said. "Cynthia does beautiful work."

Sylvia snorted. "I'm the Governor of the Zuni people, white whore," Sylvia sneered, "and I don't need your pity or your rags."

Before Shannon could open her mouth to make a reply, Sylvia stumbled forward and dumped her glass of red wine all over the front of Shannon's beautiful dress. She jumped back with a gasp and stumbled into Sam as she tried to brush the red wine from the beautiful leather dress.

"What the hell did you do, Sylvia?" Sam demanded of his grinning mother as Shannon dashed toward the French doors to try and clean as much wine as she could off the dress in an effort to save it. Tears of rage and frustration filled her eyes, and all Shannon could think was that she was glad they'd gotten pictures before this happened.

"She's a damned divorcee," Sylvia sneered in a loud voice. "She had no business wearing a white dress that represents the virginity and purity of the bride coming to her husband's bed."

Sam just shook his head as he stormed away after Shannon. He found her in the bathroom with a wet washcloth, trying to clean the wine from the front of her dress and tears rolling down her face. "I'm so sorry, baby," he said as he began unlacing her sleeves. "Let's get you out of this, and I'll take it to a leather guy I know to see if he can clean it up."

He moved to unlace the back. "You look so beautiful today, and I'm so proud to be your husband."

Shannon took off the dress, turned, and wrapped her arms around Sam's neck. "It's just a dress I only planned to wear once," she said, "and the photographer got plenty of pictures before Governor Sylvia did her thing to protest your choice of wives."

Outside Samuel glared at Sylvia. "That was a childish thing to do, Madam Governor, and I'm disappointed in you."

"And I'm disappointed that you don't see this terrible marriage for the shameful betrayal of his people that it is, Samuel," Sylvia snapped.

I don't see it as any sort of betrayal when they love one

another, and they make one another happy the way they do. Don't you want to see our son happy, Sylvy?"

Sylvia snorted. "Happiness is a ridiculous bullshit concept I have no faith in."

Samuel studied Sylvia's face. "And would you have called my marriage to a woman in China traitorous to my race?

Her face went suddenly pale. "You married in China?" she gasped. "I never married in all the time you were gone."

"My sweet Li was carrying my child," he said. "Marrying her was the honorable thing to do that I missed out on with you."

"Will you be bringing her here from China at some point?" Sylvia asked uneasily.

"She died giving birth to our daughter," Samuel said.

"Oh," Sylvia sneered. "I'm sorry. Does Sam know he has a little sister in China?"

Samuel shook his head, "The commandant of the camp crushed her skull against the concrete wall minutes after she was born because she wasn't born of a Chinese father and had red skin."

"Oh, my God," Sylvia gasped. "I'm so sorry, Samuel. How could a human do that to an innocent baby?"

"It's why it breaks my old heart to hear you spout your racist rhetoric, Sylvy. It brings back the sight of that man crushing my baby girl's skull against a wall because her skin was red and not yellow."

"I'm so very sorry, Samuel," Sylvia said. "I'll try to be better for you."

"And does that include your new daughter-in-law?"

Sylvia rolled her eyes." I don't think there's any chance of redeeming that relationship now, Samuel."

Samuel shrugged his shoulders. "You won't know until you try, and I fear you've done irreparable damage to your relationship with our son with that hateful stunt you played today after the woman bought these beautiful clothes for you to wear to this wedding." He shook his head. "You destroyed her wedding dress, for God's sake, Sylvy. I'm having a hard time forgiving you for that. I'm not certain she or our son ever will."

"I lost my head, Samuel. She stole him from me, and I don't know that I can ever forgive her for that."

Sam walked up behind them. "And I will never forgive you, Sylvia. You've done some mean, hateful things in your life before but destroying her dress on her wedding day was unforgivable, so please remove yourself from her property, my presence, and my life. I will never speak your name or think about you again with anything but hatred and disgust." He turned and stormed away.

"Did you hear that, Samuel," Sylvia said with tears brimming in her eyes. "That whore has turned him against me."

"No, Sylvia," Samuel said, "this is all your doing, and I have to agree with our son. You went way too far, this time with your racial hatred and pigheadedness."

"I remember when you thought we needed to do whatever we could to get back at our white oppressors, Samuel," Sylvia said with her eyes narrowed. "What happened to that beautiful rage?"

"I was nineteen years old, Sylvia, and had just been forced into a war I wanted no part of, but I went away, and I grew up."

"Well, Samuel," Sylvia said, "I stayed here, raised my son alone, and had to watch the white men come on our land, take our children to put in their schools where they tried to take their heritage from them and change their names to shame them. They tried to take Samuel, but I hid him away with some others, Sylvia said. "The bastards came and raped our prettiest girls and turned them into whores in their brothels for their white friends to screw, beat, and defile in the most depraved fashions." Tears streamed down Sylvia's aged face.

She took a deep breath. "I was one of those girls, Samuel until I managed to escape and return to my baby, so I have plenty of reasons to hate the white scum who've made it their missions to destroy our people, Samuel, and please don't ask me to apologize for my feelings."

Shannon walked up behind the older couple. Her anger had cooled, and when she heard Sylvia's words, she wanted to weep for what she'd gone through. "I'm sorry you had to go through that, Sylvia," she said softly, "but I wasn't the one who did those things and hate men like that more than you can know. Please don't lump me in with them just because of the shade of my skin." She took a breath. "My father's family came from the south, but I've never owned a slave and never would. Would you call me a Confederate just because members of my family were a century and a half ago?" She grinned. "If you do, then I think you should know I have Cherokee blood in my veins from my mother's side of the family. Her great grandmother was a Cherokee woman who married a Scottish trapper in Kentucky back in the nineteenth century."

Samuel smiled and swept Shannon up in his arms. "You see, Sylvy, this Daughter of my Heart is a sister as well."

Sylvia rolled her tear-filled brown eyes. "That just means her ancient grandmother was a race traitor to her people too."

"No." Shannon said with a deep sigh, "It means she was a survivor just like you and I, Sylvia." Shannon extended her hand. "Do you think we can call for a truce here?" she asked with a wink at Samuel, "because I think the Father of my Heart would like you to be my mother."

Sylvia's head jerked to stare at Samuel, who'd dropped to his knees in the sandy soil. He took Sylvia's trembling hand and slipped a modest ring much like the one Shannon wore crafted by Doc. "Governor," Samuel said with Sam and Shannon looking on, "would you do this old man the honor of becoming my wife so I might legitimize my son?"

Sylvia stared at the ring on her finger and wrapped her arms around Samuel's neck. "I've waited to hear those words for nearly sixty years, Samuel Broken Feather, and I love you as much today as I did when we first kissed after the rodeo."

Samuel winked at his son. "I told you that day in the photo you have was the best day of my life." Then he kissed his bride-to-be, who wept on his shoulder as the wedding guests who remained cheered.

Sam smiled and kissed Shannon. "I think we both have many more best days to come.

EPILOGUE

S am and Shannon led the four-year-old boy into the cabin and took him to the room Sam had added onto the back. "This will be your room now, Amos," Sam told him as the little boy stared around the space Shannon had decorated with race cars. They walked back into the living room together after the little boy had crawled up onto the race car bed and jumped around for a few minutes to test it out.

"Are you hungry?" Shannon asked the little boy as Sylvia and Samuel walked into the cabin.

"Of course he's hungry," Sylvia said with a broad grin, "he's four, and he's a boy. They're always hungry or thirsty. Take my word for it, daughter."

The child stared up at Sylvia with his lip beginning to quiver. "Now look what you've done, Sylvy," Samuel scolded. "He probably thinks you're one of those shrews from the orphanage come to take him back.

Sam kneeled before the child. "This is your grandpa," Sam said, pointing to Samuel, and that is your grandma. They live on the other end of the property and will be around a good bit of the time."

"Do you like horses, Amos?" Samuel asked.

"I like race cars," the little boy said. "I have racecars in my room. Wanna see?" he asked, holding out his hand to Samuel.

"I sure do," Samuel said and took the little boy's outstretched hand. They began to walk toward the bedroom when the child stopped and turned to Sylvia. "You wanna see the race cars too, Grandma?"

Sylvia smiled with tears brimming in her eyes. "I certainly do, young man," she said and hurried to join them.

Shannon went to the oven, where a large pan of Lil' Smokies wrapped in croissant dough sat warming for the occasion. She took out the pan, transferred some to a tray, added a bowl of bar-b-que sauce, and carried them to the living room.

"You spoil that old man," Sam chided her playfully.

"As if I don't spoil you as well," she said and gave him a deep kiss.

Sam grinned. "Let's keep it clean, woman. We have a youngster living here now."

Shannon smiled toward the bedroom, where she heard Amos in animated chatter with Samuel and Sylvia. "It sounds like they're both getting into the grandparent thing."

"And are you ready to get into the parent thing? Neither of us are exactly spring chickens."

They'd had this conversation before. Was it right to give a child parents the ages of other children's grandparents? They would both be close to eighty by the time Amos went off to college. Would that be fair to him?

The woman at the orphanage had suggested they consider adopting an older child, but they'd both said they preferred a younger child they could raise together and get to know rather than trying to wrangle a teenager right out of the gate. When they saw Amos for the first time, they both fell in love with him and wanted to take him home that very day, but had to wait for background checks, home inspections, and paperwork before officially calling Amos Samuel Broken Feather their son. He was here now, though, and Shannon knew he was going to make their lives complete.

Dear reader,

We hope you enjoyed reading *Tribal Law* Please take a moment to leave a review, even if it's a short one. Your opinion is important to us.

Discover more books by Lori Beasley Bradley at https://www. nextchapter.pub/authors/lori-beasley-bradley

Want to know when one of our books is free or discounted? Join the newsletter at http://eepurl.com/bqqB3H

Best regards,

Lori Beasley Bradley and the Next Chapter Team

You might also like:

Dolly by Lori Beasley Bradley

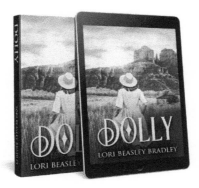

To read the first chapter for free, please head to:
https://www.nextchapter.pub/books/dolly

Tribal Law
ISBN: 978-4-86750-506-9

Published by
Next Chapter
1-60-20 Minami-Otsuka
170-0005 Toshima-Ku, Tokyo
+818035793528

6th June 2021

Lightning Source UK Ltd.
Milton Keynes UK
UKHW011827170621
385713UK00001B/175

9 784867 505069